The Secret

Nancy Rue

PUBLISHING
Colorado Springs, Colorado

THE SECRET
Copyright © 1996 by Nancy N. Rue
All rights reserved. International copyright secured.

Library of Congress Cataloging-in-Publication Data
Rue, Nancy N.
    The secret / Nancy Rue.
        p.   cm.—(Christian heritage series, the Salem years ; 6)
    Summary: Twelve-year-old Josiah and his sister draw closer together as they help to
solve the problems within their Puritan community in Salem in 1691.
    ISBN 1-56179-443-0
    [1. Puritan—Fiction. 2. Brothers and sisters—Fiction. 3. Christian life—Fiction. 4.
Salem (Mass.)—History—Colonial period, ca. 1600–1775—Fiction.] I. Title. II. Series:
Rue, Nancy N. Christian heritage series, the Salem years ; bk. 6.
PZ7.R88515Se   1996
[Fic]—dc20   95-25700
                                               CIP
                                             AC

Published by Focus on the Family Publishing,
Colorado Springs, Colorado 80995
Distributed in the U.S.A. and Canada by Word Books, Dallas, Texas

Focus on the Family books are available at special quantity discounts when purchased in
bulk by corporations, organizations, churches, or groups. Special imprints, messages, or
excerpts can be produced to meet your needs. For more information, write: Special Sales,
Focus on the Family Publishing, 8605 Explorer Dr., Colorado Springs, CO 80920; or call
(719) 531-3400 and ask for the Special Sales Department.

Editor: Keith Wall
Cover Design: Bradley Lind
Cover Illustration: Jeff Haynie

Printed in the United States of America

96 97 98 99 00/10 9 8 7 6 5 4 3 2 1

For my father, William Naylor . . .
As Josiah's papa did for him,
mine showed me what it truly is to be a Christian

Chapter One

You scrape the knife across the flint, over and over, and you should be able to start a fire.

That was what his friend Ezekiel Porter had told him.

But Josiah Hutchinson frowned at the flint he held in his hand, which had so far refused to give him so much as a spark. "Twelve years old," he muttered to himself, "and I can't even use a flint."

He stuffed the rock and the tiny knife into his whistle pouch and plucked a dandelion stem to chew. From where he sat on Hathorne's Hill, his eyes scanned Salem Village below. It seemed to be napping in the Massachusetts heat.

Suddenly, his eye caught on someone who wasn't sleeping away the afternoon. Josiah got up on his knees to watch the figure that darted along the base of the hill with skirts hiked up, and his face slowly eased into a smile.

There you are, Hope Hutchinson! he wanted to shout to her. *I have you now. You won't escape me this time!*

But he didn't say a word as he tossed aside the dandelion stem and scrambled to his feet. The clover was soft between his bare toes, and any other time he would have stopped to roll in a patch or two. But not when he had his sister almost within reach.

Hope seemed to be headed for the bank of the Ipswich River. Josiah trailed her like a hunter tracking a deer, sliding easily behind poplar trees and blackberry bushes and squinting to keep her white cap and dark curls in sight.

So this is what you've been doing every day! Josiah said to himself, pointing a finger at her in his mind. *It's sure you're going to try swimming in the river—and, of course, you don't want Mama and Papa to know it.* He and Hope both knew that the rules of the Puritan church forbade anyone to immerse themselves completely in water, although Josiah had done it more times than he would ever admit, even to Hope.

'Tis lucky for you I'm here to rescue you when you find yourself floundering, Josiah thought smugly.

But Hope didn't pull off her shoes and pull up her long, brown skirt for a wade in the Ipswich. Once she reached the bank, her steps turned northward, and Josiah frowned as he slipped behind a rock to watch her path. There was nothing up there but Hathorne's Great Swamp on one side of the road and Deacon Edward Putnam's farm on the other.

If she thinks she's going to swim in the swamp, she has a surprise coming, Josiah thought as he crept along the bank. *There's naught but swamp grass and snakes there.* He snickered to himself. *You'll be tangled up or bitten, Hope, and then I'll have to save you sure.*

That was a delicious thought for Josiah as he continued to stalk her along the side of the river. He and Hope were friends as well as siblings. Puritan children had few people to stick up for them in 1691. They were expected to behave like adults, and mistakes weren't treated lightly. He and Hope had learned to be each other's allies in everything. They told each other everything—until recently.

Since you turned 14, Josiah thought, *it's as if you suddenly have secrets I can't know about.*

As Hope reached the wide part in the river, Josiah couldn't smother a smile. It looked as if he were about to find out what at least one of those secrets was.

Hope hesitated for a minute and swiveled her head around as if she were unsure what to do next. She turned so far that Josiah had to dive into the underbrush, and he nearly slithered into the river as his feet hit the ground. He held his breath and watched, but Hope went on. She hadn't seen him, and it was sure she hadn't heard him. A bad fever a year ago last spring had left her partly deaf. Josiah had become her ears, as she often said.

Josiah bristled at the thought of that. Lately, she had been disappearing during their rare free hours and coming home breathless, tight-lipped, and starry-eyed—and without a word of explanation for Josiah. So much for being her ears, or anything else for that matter.

Josiah was so engrossed in his thoughts that he almost missed Hope's next move. Gathering up her long, bulky skirts almost to her knees, she picked her way across one of the stretches of marshy ground that plagued Putnam property until she found a high spot.

She looks like she's *following someone, too,* Josiah told himself as he looked around for a place to hide. It wasn't going to be easy in this piece of swampland, unless he crouched down in the water. Josiah rolled up his breeches and squatted carefully at the edge of the bog.

I needn't have worried about her turning 'round and seeing me, Josiah thought. *She has eyes only for what she's looking at yonder.*

But what *was* she looking at? What was there to see except bulrush, stagnant water, and Edward Putnam's miserable farm?

Josiah squirmed and looked around nervously. It wasn't his favorite thing to do—hang around Putnam property, except Joseph's, that is. Joseph Putnam was his teacher, and the only man he looked up to more was his own father. But Joseph was half brother to the four older Putnams—Thomas, Nathaniel, John, and Edward—and no one hated Josiah's family more than they did.

Josiah had never learned where the feud had started, but ever since he could remember, the Putnam brothers, and, of course, their four sons, had been his family's enemies. Josiah always shivered when he thought about the trouble Jonathon, Richard, Eleazer, and Silas Putnam had caused his friends and him over the last year. In fact, he shivered now. What was Hope doing hovering around Putnam land?

Josiah watched her as she carefully stepped closer to the edge of the farm and craned her neck as if to see something important. Perhaps it wasn't so dangerous, really. Only Silas

Putnam, Edward's 14-year-old son, would be around. Jonathon, Eleazer, and Richard Putnam were still in Salem Town, being punished for what they had done to Hope last spring. Holding a knife to Hope's neck for several hours had earned the boys five days in the stocks.

If she had been standing in front of him, Josiah would have shaken his head at her. *Didn't you learn anything from that?* he would have said to her. *Just because Silas wasn't part of it doesn't mean he's not still a Putnam. And their fathers—they would still find a way to get you for trespassing!*

Josiah jerked his neck anxiously and slapped at a fly that buzzed around his ear. Secret or no secret, maybe it was time to grab Hope by the wrist and drag her out of there. She would put up a squall, but at least she wouldn't end up in the stocks.

Josiah almost stood to slosh toward her when movement caught the corner of his eye. It caught Hope's eye, too, for Josiah heard her gasp softly. She lifted her chin as if she were straining to see, and Josiah strained with her. What could she be looking at on Edward Putnam's farm?

Then Josiah gasped, too, though not softly. He clapped a hand over this mouth and silently thanked God that no one could hear him. Coming across the meadow with a shovel in his hand was Silas Putnam. Josiah shrank down. He could feel the water seeping into the seat of his breeches, but he didn't care. He would rather feel that than Silas's shovel coming down on the top of his head. Or see it coming down on Hope's.

Josiah chewed his lip and watched his sister. Surely, Silas would be able to see her if he just looked up. He probably wouldn't come after her. He had never been as mean and violent as his cousins. But he *was* a Putnam. His wide face would turn the color of a giant strawberry, and he would scream for his father. Then before Josiah could even get to Hope, the place would be crawling with Putnams, all wagging their big heads, shouting accusations, and dragging everyone into court.

Josiah's thoughts smacked to a halt. It was happening—right now. Silas Putnam stopped to lean on his shovel and look over the landscape in front of him . . . and his eyes lit on Hope.

He has to see her, Josiah thought wildly. *She's almost right in front of him, with nothing to hide her. And she must see him looking at her. Why doesn't she run?*

Josiah wanted to run himself, but he wasn't going to leave Hope. He had done that once before, and he was sure he'd never forgive himself for that. He looked around for the best way to get to her—and then he stopped. Silas Putnam was still standing there, hands on his shovel, looking at Hope. And smiling.

Josiah tore his gaze from Silas and planted it on Hope. She was crouched in her place on a high spot in the marsh, smiling back. Josiah's eyes jolted back to Silas, where the grin was still spread across his face like a smear of butter on a slice of bread. Everything on the marsh seemed to go still—the breeze, the flies, even the swamp grass itself. A Putnam and a Hutchinson were smiling at each other, and for that, everything else paused in awe.

Then just as suddenly, the air was split by a shrill bark from the direction of the farmhouse.

"Silas!" a man's voice cried.

It was Edward Putnam, and his bulbous head comically appeared over a rise in the ground like a gopher popping its head out of a hole. But Josiah wasn't laughing. He had to get out of there, and so did Hope.

Hope, however, was way ahead of him. As soon as Silas turned to listen to his father, she snatched at her hem and skittered off, still going north. Josiah took one step to follow her and sank to his knees with a splash into the murky water.

"What was that?" Edward Putnam yelped.

Josiah heard him and held his breath.

"I heard nothing, sir," Silas said.

Lowering himself into the water, Josiah lay on his stomach so that only his head stuck above its surface. Three high clumps of grass were all that separated him from Edward Putnam's suspicious peering.

"It's sure I heard something. Treading on my land before I can get the ditch dug, they are."

"'Twas probably naught but a frog," Silas said, and he gave a weak laugh.

"You just this minute said you heard nothing!"

Josiah could almost imagine Edward Putnam's face going crimson as he shouted. He was the funniest looking of the Putnams, with his huge skull and narrow shoulders. He was like a snake with a gigantic head.

"Ach. If it's trespassers—" But Edward stopped. "We've naught to do anything about it now. You must come with me to Salem Town. Your cousins are coming home today."

"Aye, sir," Silas said.

"We've much to decide now, we Putnams," Edward said as they moved together toward the house.

Josiah lifted his head cautiously and watched them go. Silas trailed behind his father like a reluctant puppy. He hadn't seemed excited at the thought of his cousins returning to Salem Village either, Josiah thought. If Hope or any of his friends—Rachel and Ezekiel Porter, or William and Sarah Proctor—had been in the stocks in Salem Town for five days, he would be overjoyed to see them come back.

As they disappeared over the rise, out of earshot, Josiah let out a relieved puff of air and looked around for Hope. He could just see her cap bouncing along the bank, going toward Indian Bridge. She didn't seem to have any mission now except to get away from Putnam property.

Josiah gritted his teeth. *I'm going to catch up to you, Hope Hutchinson,* he thought, *and find out what you were doing here in the first place.*

Gingerly, he picked his way out of the swamp and waded to high ground. *And you'll pay for all the time I spent in this disgusting water,* he added in his mind. He sat down on a rock to squeeze some water from his shirt, still watching Hope move up the riverbank like a vanishing white dot. In a minute, she would be out of sight. Josiah stretched his legs and started to stand. Suddenly, a pain like the lashing of a whip went through his left calf.

Josiah reached down to grab it, just in time to see the snake recoil. Its brown skin, laced with diamond markings, drew back like a spring, and an angry rattling came from its tail.

From out of nowhere, someone screamed, and Josiah tried to back over the rock. The snake's diamond-shaped head rose high in the air, and Josiah fell backward and tumbled over the boulder. And all the while, someone was still screaming.

It wasn't until Josiah had pulled himself up that he realized it was he himself who was howling in terror. The pain burned his calf, and almost at once, his leg turned to lead—hot lead he had to drag to get farther from the marsh. Up the riverbank, the white cap had all but vanished, but Josiah cried out to it until he thought his lungs would burst.

"Hope!" he screamed over and over. "Hope, help me!"

But of course, she couldn't hear him.

Chapter Two

As his final call to Hope croaked lifelessly from his lips, Josiah sank to the ground again. The pain in his calf was moving like a wildfire up his leg, and he was sure he wouldn't be able to move.

But he had to. He'd just been bitten by a rattlesnake. A big rattlesnake. He had to get home. He had to get to Papa. His father would know what to do.

Josiah tried to stand up, but his leg crumpled under him like a wad of parchment. Josiah clutched it and tried to gather his thoughts, which were scattering in his head in frightened bits and pieces he couldn't collect.

I'll never get home—it's too far. . . .
Mama will have herbs—she'll know what to do. . . .
But I can't get there—I can't walk. . . .
Crawl—try to crawl. . . .

Josiah snatched at that last thought and dug his fingers

10

into the ground. With a heave of both arms and a push from his good leg, he could scoot himself along. Gnawing fiercely at his lip, Josiah clawed and pulled and dragged. After several yards, he collapsed in the dirt, and his panicked thoughts collided with each other.

I'll never get home this way. I'll die first. Snakebites kill you—they kill you. . . .

The pain was pumping all the way to his hip now, and Josiah grabbed at the ground again. He had to crawl, and he had to think straight. Where could he go for help before his thoughts stopped completely? Who would help him on this Putnam land?

Joseph Putnam!

At the thought of his teacher in his big, white house just at the other end of Hathorne's Great Swamp, Josiah's head cleared and his arms scooted him forward again. If he could just get that far, Joseph could get Papa. He would be all right. . . .

Sweat poured down the sides of Josiah's face, bringing trails of curls with it. His breathing squeezed out in rasping gasps as he lurched and pulled, lurched and pulled. Halfway past the swamp, he stopped, and tears joined the sweat that drenched his face. He couldn't feel anything below his waist except the searing, fiery pain.

I'll just rest a minute, and then I'll go on, he told himself. *I'll go on to Joseph Putnam's.*

But he could hardly hear his own thoughts.

Nor did he hear the hoofbeats until they were almost on top of him. Josiah squinted up through the sweat that dropped from his eyebrows. It had to be a Putnam. This was their land, and they seldom traveled two feet without their horses. But surely even Thomas wouldn't let him die here. Surely, he would take him to Joseph's—

"Josiah!" a voice cried.

Josiah almost cried with it. Everything before his eyes was blurred, but the oak-colored hair of Joseph Putnam burned through. Suddenly, Joseph was upon him.

"Josiah, what's happened? Good heavens, you're burning up!"

Josiah tried to move his lips to say "snake," but they stuck stubbornly together, and his tongue lay thickly in the bottom of his mouth. He dragged a heavy arm against his leg.

"Your leg? What is it?" Josiah felt Joseph turning him over and sliding his smooth hand down his calf.

"Merciful Lord, help us!" he heard Joseph Putnam say, before the world slipped away.

Merciful Lord, help us.

The leaf of plantain, Constance. Draws out the deadly poison. Merciful Lord, please help us. Now bugloss soup. When he awakes, bugloss soup.

The widow taught me those. Plantain has the leaves toward the bottom of the stems, Big Squirrel. And spikes of tiny, greenish flowers. Bugloss has blue flowers and hairy stems.

Slowly, the thoughts untangled themselves. Josiah could tell that some of them were in his own head and some were coming from fuzzy voices all around him.

"His eyes are fluttering, Joseph," said a soft voice.

"Aye, thank God," said another one, bright and crisp.

"Amen to that. Josiah, can you hear me?"

The last voice was deep and commanding. Josiah forced

his eyes open and searched the haze above him for his father. "Josiah, can you hear me?" Papa said again.

Josiah was afraid to try to speak. What if his tongue wouldn't move? Or his lips—ever again? Carefully, slowly, he tested his head to see if it would nod.

"Ah! We've our captain back, eh?" Joseph Putnam cried.

"Shall we try the soup now, Joseph?" the soft voice said.

Joseph Putnam must have nodded, for he heard Constance Putnam walking out of the room. Things were beginning to come into focus, and Josiah searched again for his father. Joseph Hutchinson sat on the edge of the soft surface Josiah was lying on. It felt smooth and cool and smelled of flowers. He must be in Joseph Putnam's house, in one of his elegant sleeping rooms.

"'Twas a snake, then, Josiah?" his father said.

Josiah nodded.

"Can you speak, boy? Try."

Even with his mind muddled, Josiah knew no one dared argue with Joseph Hutchinson—including those who were crawling back from the edge of death.

Josiah coaxed his lips into motion. "Aye, sir," he said slowly. "A rattlesnake, I think. A big one."

"You were right, Joseph," Papa said to Joseph Putnam. "And it's good you were, or he'd have been gone sure."

"God was surely on our side. The big snakes, the old ones, won't let out all their venom on such big prey as you, Josiah, because they know they can't swallow all of you, eh? They just want to scare you away. We can thank God—and the Indians."

"That was an Indian cure you used?" Papa asked.

"Aye." Joseph Putnam brought his handsome face with its crisp eyes close to Josiah's. "Don't move that leg, Captain. We've a poultice of—"

"Plantain," Josiah mumbled. "To draw out the poison."

"Goodman Hutchinson, it's a wonder your son didn't pull a plant of plantain out of the ground right where he was bitten and heal himself!"

"Where *were* you when the snake bit you, Josiah?" Papa said. "It's sure you were soaking wet when Joseph found you."

Josiah's eyes were clear enough now that he could see his father's own blue eyes boring in on him. Under their sandy, hooded brows, they could always shoot right into Josiah and come out knowing the truth, whether Josiah told it or not. Therefore, it was best to do so.

But before Josiah could get his slow mouth moving, Constance Putnam pushed the door open and ambled in with a tray of bugloss soup and hot tea.

"We can thank the Indians once again," Joseph said.

Joseph Putnam dazzled a smile at his young wife, but Josiah switched his gaze to the soup and riveted it there. Constance was going to have their first baby soon, and Josiah had a hard time looking at her round belly as she waddled about. He wasn't sure it was proper to look at a woman who was going to have a baby, and he could never do it without feeling his cheeks flame redder than a Putnam's head.

But at least this time he could be thankful to her for one thing. She had saved him from having to answer his father's question.

"'Tis too bad you didn't catch that snake and bring him home," Joseph Putnam said to Josiah. "The Indians say if a woman who is with child drinks snake's blood, things will go easier with her when the baby comes."

Constance gasped softly, and Joseph Putnam chuckled. "I was only fooling, Constance," he said. "You've naught to worry about me dropping the blood of a rattler into your stew."

Josiah had to smile. Most Puritans were a somber lot, seldom laughing, and even more seldom making jokes. Joseph Putnam was an exception to that rule, and it was one of the things Josiah loved best about him.

"What say you, Joseph?" Papa said. "A few days in bed, off this leg?"

"Aye, at least that. And a new poultice several times a day until we're sure we've gotten all the poison out." Young Putnam nudged Josiah playfully and wiggled his eyebrows. "And plenty of this soup, which you love, eh, Captain?"

Josiah wrinkled his nose, but a glance targeted at him by his father quickly brought the spoon to his lips. Anything to keep from arousing any more questions. His father sighed heavily and stood up, and Josiah noticed for the first time that the broad shoulders Joseph Hutchinson was known for were sagging.

"You should get some rest yourself, my friend," Joseph Putnam said to him. "It's near midnight."

Josiah looked up at the window in surprise. It was dark, and he could hear the night crickets in chorus outside. It had been just after noon when he had started following Hope, and now it was the middle of the night. They had worked a long time to save him. He dug guiltily into his soup.

"Aye, Joseph," his father was saying. "It's a wonder any of us sleeps at all, even without snakebites."

"You're thinking of the church, eh?" Putnam said.

"Aye, constantly, when I'm not worrying over the sawmill, or the crops, or your half brothers. . . ."

"Or Reverend Parris," Joseph said.

Papa nodded wearily and ran his big hand across the back of his thick hair. Josiah noticed in the light of the lamp that a few strands of gray had crept into his father's sandy-colored waves.

"Are the Porters still bent on running Reverend Parris out of Salem Village?" Joseph Putnam asked.

"Nay. At least that's what Giles and Benjamin tell me. They say they've stopped all thoughts of any plot to take him down."

Josiah watched as Joseph Putnam's eyebrows shot up. "And you have reason to doubt them still? You've been friends with the Porters for a long time."

"Aye," Papa replied, "and that makes it hard for me to believe they would be up to any more mischief, after what Giles tried to do last spring." Papa put his hand on Joseph Putnam's shoulder. "I know Giles is your brother-in-law, Joseph, and I don't mean to cast a shadow on your wife's brother. But you know he tried to pull me into reclaiming the property my father gave for the church and the parsonage so Parris would be left on the street."

"Aye, I remember. But he's promised, Joseph."

"Aye, and I'm trying to trust him. But in the meantime, I think we must find other ways to soften this quarrel that constantly exists in the church."

"We've tried all the things I know of," Joseph Putnam said.

Josiah's father crossed his arms over his big chest as he paced to the window. He stood looking out, blocking the moonlight, before he turned to Joseph Putnam again. "All but one," he said.

"And that is?"

"Sitting down with all the Putnams—and Parris—and praying together for God's hand to set the pieces right. It's sure I'd like to get back to worshiping again, instead of fighting."

Josiah listened without making a sound. He knew better than to interject his opinion.

Joseph Putnam folded his hands and rested his chin on the tips of his two index fingers, a gesture Josiah had seen him make many times before. It meant he was thinking— seriously.

"You know all the Putnams would be suspicious of such a suggestion," he said, "as would Parris himself, since he agrees with whatever they tell him is truth."

"And I agree with what God tells me is truth," Joseph Hutchinson said firmly. He shook his head. "I have naught to do but try."

A gentle smile spread over Joseph Putnam's face, and he turned to Josiah. "He's a good man, your father," he said. "We'd all do well to be like him."

Papa tossed his head and avoided their eyes as he reached down to scoop Josiah into his arms. They felt like iron bands around him, and Josiah knew Joseph Putnam was right. His father was a good man, and a strong man. If anyone could save the church in Salem Village, long torn by quarrels and jealousy, it was Joseph Hutchinson.

Mama and Hope were waiting, white-faced, in the kitchen when Papa carried Josiah into the house and directly upstairs to the room he shared with Hope.

"He shall sleep here until he's well," Papa announced, passing Josiah's cot and setting him down on Hope's curtained bed. Josiah didn't have to look at Hope to know she was drilling him with her eyes.

"Joseph says he's to have another poultice put on before he sleeps," Papa said.

"I can do that if you wish, Papa," Hope said.

Josiah looked at her quickly. Her black eyes were shining. *She's much more interested in getting information from me than she is in taking care of me*, he thought. *Well, I have some information to get from her, too. It's sure she owes me that.*

Deborah Hutchinson ran a cool hand over Josiah's forehead and looked into his face with her dark, compassionate eyes. They were so much like Hope's and yet so different. Hers never snapped with anger or twinkled with mischief like Hope's. They were almost always as soft and warm as they were at that moment. Mama was like a deer. Hope was like a fox.

"I thank the Lord you're safe, Josiah," Mama said quietly. "Before you sleep, see that you thank Him as well."

"Aye, Mama," Josiah said.

She brushed her lips across his forehead, and Josiah felt his cheeks burn, but only a little. His mother could kiss him, because she was his mother. But kissing wasn't something he liked to think about for long.

Hope returned with two bowls on a tray, one containing a plantain poultice and the other holding something pinkish that made Josiah wrinkle his nose. As soon as Deborah

Hutchinson closed the door behind her, Hope pounced.

"Where were you that you got yourself into a tangle with a snake, Josiah Hutchinson?" she demanded as she hastily pulled off the old poultice and plopped it onto the tray.

"Hey! Be careful!" Josiah said. "Must you be so rough?"

"And must you avoid my question? Where were you this afternoon?"

"I could ask you the same thing," Josiah said. His snappy reply earned him more rough treatment, causing more pain. "Ouch! You're pressing too hard."

"Don't be a ninny . . . and hold still," Hope said. She pressed the poultice into place and wiped her hands on her apron. "Why would you be asking me questions? All I have is some heat rash, which I can take care of with a little yarrow. I'm not the one who nearly got himself killed."

Josiah watched as she dipped her hand into the bowl of pink paste made from the leaves and flowers of the yarrow weed. "Well, you just might get yourself killed if you keep hanging about Edward Putnam's farm," he said.

She stopped, yarrow dripping from her palm, and stared at him. "How did you know I was at Putnam's farm? You were spying on me, Josiah Hutchinson!"

She slapped the paste intended for her heat rash back into the bowl and hurriedly dried her hands so she could plant them on her hips.

"Before you begin to lecture me about being someplace I was not supposed to be," Josiah said, "just remember, you were, too." He had seen that stern posture—hands on hips, clenched jaw, tilted chin—many times before, and he wasn't going to give her a chance to get the upper hand.

But Hope drew her face close to Josiah's and scowled. "It is none of your business what I was doing there," she said. Her lips were tight as she spoke. "And I'll thank you not to pry into my business by following me." She smirked down at his leg. "Though it looks like I won't have to worry about that for a while, now, will I?"

"You should thank me for being there!" Josiah cried.

"*Thank* you?"

"Aye, if Edward Putnam had caught you out there smiling like a ninny at his son, you would have needed me to—"

"Shut it, Josiah!"

"I won't!"

"Shhh! You'll bring Papa in here!"

Josiah jerked upright on the bed, and his head spun. "Maybe I should! Have you gone mad, Hope? The Putnams already showed you how dangerous they can be. And if Edward finds you out there, he'll have you—or Papa—thrown in jail for trespassing."

Hope jerked her head back. "The Putnams will never try to hurt us again. I'm sure they haven't enjoyed five days in the stocks, and they know we'll tell on them if they try something again. Besides, I've no need to worry about Silas."

"Why not?"

She started to answer, but just as quickly, she clamped her lips shut and picked up the tray. "You need your rest if you're going to get well," she said crisply. She shot him a dark look. "I shall sleep downstairs on the settle, since you have my bed."

After she was gone, Josiah lay staring at the curtains that closed him into what was usually Hope's little world. *I wish I knew what she thought about in here,* he said to himself. But before he could even begin to guess, he felt sleep overtaking him.

"I hope you know I'm thankful to you, Lord," he muttered as he drifted off. "I'm just too tired to tell you."

osiah tried to climb out of bed as soon as his eyes opened the next morning, but one step onto the plank floor sent his head spinning and the pain shooting up his leg.

"I don't see why you're so anxious to get up," Hope said from the doorway. "I would be happy to lie in bed for three days instead of drawing the water and scrubbing the linen and weeding the vegetables—"

"Three days!" Josiah cried.

"'Tis what Papa said last night."

Josiah cringed as she put a tray of baked apples and milk in front of him.

"Was he angry that I won't be able to do my work?" he said.

Hope's black eyes sparkled. "Aye. 'Tis very likely you'll be whipped the moment you're able to get out of bed."

22

Josiah wrinkled his nose at her and picked up his spoon. Unlike most Puritans, Joseph Hutchinson didn't whip his children. He was moving away from many of the harsher Puritan rules—while, he often pointed out, many of the Puritans who kept the rules seemed to be moving away from God.

"It's sure *you'll* be whipped, too, then," Josiah said to Hope. "Once I tell Papa where I found you yesterday."

The sparkle disappeared from Hope's eyes, and she flounced to the door. "I told you to mind your own business!" she said. The wall shook as she slammed the door behind her.

But Josiah couldn't mind his own business. He lay miserably on Hope's bed for most of the morning, tossing the mystery around in his head. Had he really seen his sister, a Hutchinson, smiling at Silas, a Putnam? Had he actually witnessed that same Putnam smiling back at her? It was certain he had. But why?

Just before noon, he heard the door slam below and footsteps running across the yard toward the road. The world was continuing on down there—without him.

Sliding carefully from the bed, Josiah held on to the bedpost and then grabbed for his cot. Stretching next for the blanket chest, he was able to hop to the window and sit down on the chest. He huffed and puffed as if he had just run across the yard in the noonday heat. But as he gazed out the window, his breathing steadied, and he stared. It was Hope who had taken flight from the Hutchinson farm, and he could see her just leaving the road and slowing down. She was about to walk right onto Reverend Parris's property.

Josiah leaned forward as far as he dared without falling out the window. He watched her look over both shoulders, just as she had done yesterday, and then head for a row of bushes that bordered the parsonage yard.

Yarrow leaves, Josiah thought. *She's gone to gather more yarrow for her heat rash.* He was about to look around for something more interesting to occupy his mind when his eyes snagged on another figure, this one running from the parsonage itself. *Betty Parris!* Josiah almost shouted.

He hadn't seen Betty Parris since the spring. Even though she was Reverend Parris's daughter, Josiah had come to consider her as good a friend as William or Ezekiel. She was thin as a new twig and had pale, almost transparent, skin from her many illnesses—and from being cooped up in that dark parsonage, Josiah reckoned. But she had been a great help to Josiah's Merry Band of friends last spring by writing and sending messages for them whenever they were needed.

Josiah sat up with a start as Betty slid behind the same bushes Hope had retreated to. Messages! His sister must be having Betty deliver messages to someone.

Why has Hope stopped telling me everything? Josiah asked himself sadly. But then he shrugged. He didn't care. Let her get herself into trouble alone if she wanted.

Josiah started to turn away from the window, but once more his eye was caught by movement in Parris's yard. This time it was coming from the direction of the minister's barn.

"What on earth?" Josiah said out loud. For strolling from the barn as if he were Reverend Parris's groom was Giles Porter.

Giles was the grandson of old Israel Porter, who had been

his father's adviser and best friend until he had died last spring. Giles was also cousin to Josiah's friend Ezekiel, but Josiah didn't consider Giles to be his friend. Although he claimed to be on the Hutchinsons' side in the conflicts over the church, Josiah had seen the charming young Giles do too many sneaky things to ever be able to trust him. Was he doing one of them now? Josiah wondered.

Why else would he be strutting across the minister's property? He and the rest of the Porters hated Reverend Parris. They only went to his village church because it was required that Puritans attend every Sunday, but Giles usually sat with his big, gray Porter eyes slanted suspiciously the entire time Samuel Parris was preaching. So what was Giles doing stepping out onto the road in front of Parris's house looking as if he'd just been inside having a friendly cup of tea?

Suddenly, Hope popped up from behind the bushes and hurried toward the road. She was so busy looking over her left shoulder to be sure no one had seen her that she nearly plowed into Giles on her right. Josiah held his breath and watched.

Hope looked startled at first. She, of course, hadn't heard Giles practically at her elbow, and the sight of him made her jerk her skirts in surprise. But as Josiah looked on, his sister's face broke into a smile, and she gave her dark curls a gentle toss. Giles, too, gave a smile, one of the smooth ones Josiah had seen him flash during uncomfortable moments when other people were doubling their fists and gritting their teeth. He had a way of charming everyone within seeing or hearing distance.

He's certainly charming Hope, Josiah thought. Josiah

squirmed in his nightshirt. Surely, Hope wasn't fooled by any story he might be telling her right now about why he was marching across Reverend Parris's yard. Josiah hoped that whatever his sister had been doing over there, she wasn't confessing it to Giles Porter.

As Giles moved on and Hope made her way back across the road toward the Hutchinson house, Josiah hobbled back to bed and pretended to be sleeping. He breathed deeply and evenly when, a few minutes later, Hope rustled up the steps and came into the room.

He heard her stop in the doorway and then quickly move toward the bed on light feet. He expected her to lean over and whisper to him, but instead she seemed to be crouching down. He slit an eye open, and then opened both eyes all the way and sat straight up. Hope was disappearing under the bed.

"What are you doing?" he said.

There was a thud and a squeal below him, and Hope backed out, red-faced, pulling a small, wooden chest with her.

"You nearly frightened me out of my wits!" she cried. "Made me bump my head, you did!"

"'Tis a strange place to have your head, if you ask me," Josiah said. "What's that?" He pointed to the chest, which Hope was dusting off with her apron on the floor beside the bed.

"Did that snakebite affect your eyes?" she said. "'Tis just what it looks like—a storage chest."

She opened the lid, and Josiah peered over it to see inside. "What is it for?" Josiah said.

"Things," Hope said primly. She reached up on the bed, where she had laid a pile of white cloth and pulled the items into her lap. Although they looked perfectly folded to Josiah, she began folding them again.

"What are those for?" he said.

"Must you ask so many questions?"

"Aye. There's naught else to do."

Hope sighed as if to answer was an effort. "They're linens," she said. "I embroidered them."

"For who?" Josiah said.

"For me."

"Why? Haven't we enough linens in the house for you?"

"Aye, in this house. These are for my own house—the one I shall have someday with my husband."

Josiah let out a loud snort. "Husband? You?"

Hope tilted her chin at him, and her eyes blazed. "Aye! Is that so hard to think of—that someday I might be married?"

Josiah started to answer, but his lips stopped before any words came out. It was hard, for sure. Hope was a girl, and some people said she was pretty, though most followed with, "But 'twould be a sin for her to become vain." But married? It seemed she had barely stopped making little baskets and fairy cradles out of milkweed pods!

"Do Mama and Papa know you're doing this?" Josiah said.

Hope gave him a look that would have withered an apple. "Yes," she said impatiently. "'Twas Mama who suggested it, and Papa who made me this." Hope held up a small, wooden trencher, carved in Joseph Hutchinson's unmistakable style with the initials HEH. Hope Elizabeth Hutchinson.

She smiled triumphantly and put the trencher carefully back into the chest.

"But you're only 14!" Josiah said.

"I wouldn't expect you to understand," Hope said as she closed the lid and slid the chest back under the bed. "You're still busy getting yourself bitten by snakes and spying on your sister."

Josiah's thoughts lurched. He had gotten so caught up in Hope's bridal treasures that he'd almost forgotten about his most recent spying. He leaned back on the pillows and crossed his arms. "I was at the window just now," he said, "and I saw you and Giles Porter, and before that—"

"I saw Giles Porter, too," Hope said. She leaned against the bed and looked at the wall, as if Giles's face had appeared there. As far as Josiah could tell, she liked what she saw. "He's a handsome thing," she said.

Josiah frowned. "Aye, perhaps on the outside—"

"All the Porters are, but I think he more so than the rest. His cheekbones aren't quite so sharp." She giggled softly. "Ezekiel's sometimes look as if they'll poke right through his skin, but not Giles's."

Josiah stared at her. His no-nonsense sister had just giggled. It may have been the first silly thing he had ever seen her do.

"I want to ask you something, Josiah," she said abruptly. She sat on the bed to face him, and her face was somber. "But you must promise not to answer like a brainless boy."

Josiah nodded.

Hope looked at her hands and then up at him. "Am I . . . I mean, do you think that I . . . through a boy's eyes, of course . . . ?"

She puffed out her cheeks and let the air go as Josiah stared at her. If he hadn't known Hope better, he would have thought she was afraid of what his answer might be. If he was ever going to find out what her new secrets were, he was going to have to be careful how he answered.

"Do you think I'm pretty?" she blurted out.

Josiah had to catch his tongue in his teeth to keep from laughing.

"Well, do you?" Hope said. The shyness was gone from her face, and her eyes were beginning to snap again.

"Aye," Josiah said quickly. "Everyone says so. Constance and Joseph, Sarah Proctor—"

"But as a *boy*, do *you* say so?"

"What does it matter who says it?" Josiah said.

Hope stood up with a jolt and yanked her cap down tighter over her curls. "I knew I shouldn't have asked you!" she said. "I just thought perhaps since you had taken to Betty Parris, you'd understand."

Josiah didn't know what that had to do with it, but Betty's name gave his memory a nudge. He wanted to ask Hope—

But it was too late. She had already marched from the room, giving the door a resounding slam as she went.

Girls are an odd lot, Josiah thought as he listened to her pound down the steps. *There's no doubt about it.* Betty Parris was the only one he knew who made any sense at all.

Slowly, Josiah grinned to himself. That was it, of course. If he could find out nothing from Hope, he could ask Betty Parris. He looked ruefully at his poulticed calf. As soon as he could, he would ask her.

✢ ✦ ✢

Chapter Four

Two more days passed before Josiah was allowed out of bed, and only then after Mama, Papa, Joseph Putnam, and Hope had all examined his leg as if it were going to fall off if he left his bed one minute too soon.

"'Tis a miracle that it healed this quickly," Joseph Putnam said. He patted Josiah's shoulder. "You're from good, sturdy stock, Captain. You've grown so much in the year since I first gave you that name, eh?"

Josiah would have enjoyed thinking back to his summer in Salem Town, exploring the ships and learning how to read and write under Joseph Putnam's teaching—if he hadn't been squirming inside his skin to be let out of bed.

"What say you, Deborah?" Joseph Hutchinson was saying to his wife. "Think you the boy is strong enough?"

Josiah looked at his mother and tried not to beg her. Deborah Hutchinson smiled her shy smile. "Aye, if there's anything he is, Joseph, it's strong as an ox."

"And foolish as a turkey," Hope mumbled near Josiah's ear. But her eyes were dancing, and Josiah guessed she had forgotten that he had been prying into her business. Good. That would keep her suspicions off him until he could question Betty Parris.

Still, even though Josiah was permitted to leave his room, it seemed as if everyone was guarding him like a newborn calf not able to walk yet.

"Careful now, Josiah. Sit you down now."

"Don't try to carry too much at once."

"'Twill be days before you're able to do *that*."

Josiah thought he would scream before they finally seemed to decide he wasn't going to collapse in his tracks and began to leave him alone. He finished what few chores he was allowed to do and found a chance to slip across the road to Betty's, his pouch filled with tiny pebbles.

Glancing casually over both shoulders to be sure Salem Village was quiet in all directions, Josiah crept behind the bushes and emptied his pouch into his hand. He didn't know how Hope had gotten Betty's attention the other day, but Josiah's usual method was to lightly toss pebbles at Betty's window until she looked down and saw him.

Except when he was confined to bed, Josiah was seldom in his room during the day, but Betty Parris seemed to spend most of her time in hers. The Parrises had two slaves from Barbados, Tituba and John Indian, who did all the work, so Betty and her cousin Abigail Williams seldom had anything to do.

Josiah suspected Betty stayed in her room to keep away

from narrow-eyed Abigail, who was as hateful to everyone as the Putnams were to the Hutchinsons. Hope had once said that Abigail was probably mean and spiteful because she was an orphan and had been taken in by the Parrises, who didn't really want her. Josiah thought it was just because she was evil, inside and out.

He tossed his last pebble and crouched behind the bushes waiting. Any minute now, Betty's wispy blonde hair would appear in the window, and she would hold up one finger to let him know she would be down in a minute. Josiah imagined her stealing invisibly past Tituba in the kitchen when he felt a wiry hand grip his shoulder.

"What are you about here, boy?" said a high-pitched male voice.

Even in the muggy heat of the afternoon, Josiah went cold all over. The hand on his shoulder and the whining voice belonged to Reverend Parris.

"What are you about here?" he asked again, even higher this time. His long, taut fingers curled into Josiah's shirt and brought him up to his feet with a yank. "Why are you skulking about in my bushes like a weasel, young Hutchinson?" He gave Josiah a shake. "Answer me, boy!"

Even if the minister had given him a chance to answer, Josiah didn't know what he would have said. If he were to tell the truth, he would have to say, "I'm here to meet your daughter and pry information from her." But that would only get Betty in trouble. He would rather be put in the stocks himself than do that.

Josiah gulped down the lump that was forming in his throat. The stocks weren't far from what could happen when you tangled with Reverend Parris. Josiah had to think of something to say, but lies didn't come into his head easily.

"Well, will you answer or shall I call for the deputy constable?" the reverend demanded. "He'll find out soon enough whether you were spying for your father!"

"My father?" Josiah burst out. "Oh, no, sir!"

"Then what—?"

Suddenly, a scream cut through Parris's words, and a chorus of cries and terrified shouts followed. They were coming from the direction of the barn, and one of them sounded to Josiah like Betty's voice.

"God in heaven preserve us!" Reverend Parris shouted.

Josiah wasn't sure whether the man ever would have gone to the barn instead of standing there crying out, but Josiah himself tore toward it with his toes digging the ground. Every one of those screaming people sounded like they were being killed.

The barn doors were open, and Reverend Parris's horse, Gussie, was halfway out. The whites of her eyes were bulging, and she was tossing her head against the harness that threatened to choke her. Behind her, Reverend Parris's wagon was tilted at a peculiar angle, and one of its wheels lay on the ground, still spinning to a stop from where it had fallen from the wagon. The axle stuck out like a broken wing.

"What's happened here?" Reverend Parris sniveled as he came up behind Josiah. The reverend's voice was winding up to its highest pitch yet.

Instead of answering, John Indian climbed out of the driver's seat and pointed solemnly to the wheel. Still clutching the side of the wagon with one hand, Tituba cried softly and held Betty against her with the other. Both she and Betty were trembling like moths.

"I shall tell you what happened, Uncle!" said a voice from the barn floor.

Josiah peeked around the broken wagon and saw Abigail for the first time. She was sprawled among the hay and horse dung, the back of her skirt halfway over her head and her fiery face covered with so much dust and straw that she looked like a scarecrow. Josiah had to turn his head to keep from laughing.

"I shall tell you!" Abigail said again. "Some evil son of Satan has been in this barn and fixed the wagon so we would all go out on the road and be killed!"

John Indian straightened up beside the axle and nodded to his master.

"It's come to this, has it?" Reverend Parris said. His voice shook. "Now they're trying to kill me and my family!"

"Who is, Papa?" said a tiny voice from the wagon.

Samuel Parris looked at Betty, and to Josiah's surprise, he reached up to take her in his arms. Betty clasped her father's neck and buried her face in it. Josiah didn't know the pinched-faced minister could show love for anyone.

"I'll tell you who, Betty Parris!" Abigail said suddenly. She struggled to stand, hay still poking out of her hair. "'Twas him!" she said, pointing her finger straight at Josiah.

Four pairs of eyes joined hers to stare at him. Only Betty's and Tituba's were filled with doubt. John Indian closed his eyes as if the matter were decided, and Reverend Parris's narrowed until Josiah thought they would disappear altogether. He surely wished *he* could disappear.

"Aye," the minister said slowly. "So that's why I found you lurking about on my property. You'd just done your villainous work, and you were waiting to see the results." Josiah shook his head as Samuel Parris brought his nose down until it was almost touching his. "You shall be punished for this, boy. But that will be nothing like the punishment you shall receive on the Judgment Day for tampering with a man of God!"

Josiah looked around wildly. Was no one going to step in and stop this madman? Tituba, perhaps, who had always been on his and Betty's side?

But Tituba was making a knot in the hem of her skirt and rocking back and forth, moaning softly. And Betty—

Josiah swallowed hard at the lump in his throat. He would never dream of speaking against his own father's word, and his father was at least reasonable. There was nothing Betty could do that wouldn't bring a high-pitched wrath upon herself.

Josiah looked at the minister, whose eyes were rimmed red with anger. "I had naught to do with it, sir. I would never . . ."

But it seemed his word meant even less than the condition of his shirt, for once again, Samuel Parris wrapped his wiry fingers around his sleeve and began to drag him roughly toward the house.

"You!" the reverend bayed at John Indian. "Get you to Thomas Putnam's and bring him here at once. He will want to know about this, and I shall need his advice."

The lump in Josiah's throat doubled in size as Reverend Parris pulled him to the front door, and the tall, black Barbados slave strode off toward the Putnams'. With the leader of the Putnam clan coming here, waving his fist and howling out threats, there was no hope for Josiah. And all because he couldn't stay out of Hope's affairs. Right now it didn't matter why she had been to Edward Putnam's or what she'd talked to Betty Parris about.

The image of Hope whispering with Betty behind the bushes suddenly froze in Josiah's mind. There had been someone else there that day, coming from the barn—coming from the Parrises' barn.

As Reverend Parris shoved Josiah into his dim, stuffy study, all Josiah could think about was Giles Porter saunter-ing away from the barn as if he'd had some business there, and then pretending to Hope that he had just happened along the road. She had been so eager to keep him from noticing where she had been that she hadn't thought to ask where he had been. But now Josiah knew.

The reverend pushed Josiah toward the desk chair and said, "With God's help, I was able to bear the stealing of my firewood and the failure of people like your father to pay their taxes so that I could survive."

Josiah looked up to see Reverend Parris pacing about the small, hot room like a penned rooster. "I could even pray for the forgiveness of those who thought to take my home away from me. But I cannot close my eyes to the attempt of murder on my family. I cannot blink at it anymore, d'y'hear? I cannot!"

There was a timid tap on the door. For a fleeting second, Josiah hoped it was Betty, come to speak good of him to her father. But it was Elizabeth Parris, the minister's frail, almost transparent wife. She peered in with eyes that always looked to Josiah like they were too big for her face. He could barely hear her voice above her husband's labored breathing.

"Samuel, what is this Abigail tells me about someone trying to murder us?" she said.

In answer, Samuel Parris jabbed a finger toward Josiah, and Elizabeth gasped.

"Why, Samuel, he's naught but a boy!" she said.

"I care not! He's a Hutchinson, and they're a dangerous lot."

She gazed at Josiah as if she were trying to find some trademark of crime on his face. He looked back at her hopefully. His own mother was quiet like this woman, but when she did speak up, his father listened to her. Maybe she had some influence on the reverend.

"Samuel, truly. . . ," Elizabeth Proctor started to say. But she stopped as the front door slammed and a booming voice rattled through the hall.

"'Tis Thomas," Samuel Parris said. He brushed past his wife, and then stopped to stab a bony finger at Josiah. "You stay right there, boy. It will go worse for you if you move so much as a muscle."

He watched for a second as if to dare Josiah to even blink, and then he dashed from the room with his mouselike wife behind him.

The door closed like a slap, and Josiah leaned back in the chair and closed his eyes to keep the tears from pooling there. He had been in twisted situations before, but this was the worst. He was being accused of murder. They were saying he had tried to kill Reverend Parris's family.

And what could he do? Accuse Giles Porter? With the back of his hand, Josiah swabbed miserably at the sweat that beaded in a chain of droplets across his forehead. Although he had seen Giles coming from the scene of the almost-crime, he had no proof. Was pointing the finger at Giles any better than what Parris was doing to him?

Josiah opened his eyes and tried to blink away the tears, but several spilled out onto his cheeks. He looked around, hoping the minister would have a handkerchief or even a pen wipe so he could get rid of the tears before anyone suspected him of crying. Especially Betty.

Carefully, Josiah lifted a few books on the desk, but there was nothing except what looked like a half-written sermon and some other official-looking papers. Josiah sniffed. Most people had to write letters and messages on pieces of bark, because paper was so scarce. Here was Reverend Parris packaging bundles of parchment together, and even sealing them with wax. The letter P rose proudly out of each wax insignia as if it stood for the king himself.

"He's in here," Reverend Parris whined from the hall. Quickly, Josiah swiped at his cheeks with the back of his hand. That would have to do for now.

The door flung open, and Thomas Putnam's big bull's head appeared, already gleaming the color of cranberries. "The Hutchinsons again, eh?"

He lunged into the room and pulled Josiah up by the front of his sweat-soaked shirt. In spite of his small shoulders, Thomas Putnam could be strong when he was angry. Josiah clutched at the man's wrists to hold on, for his feet had been jerked off the floor.

"My son and nephews went to jail and suffered humiliation in the stocks for something your sister accused them of—

something which everyone in this village knows they never did." He gave Josiah an angry shake that jerked his head back. "I intend to see that what you suffer is much, much worse." He let go of Josiah and sent him tumbling toward the door. "Come, Mr. Parris," he said. "We shall take this boy to Joseph Hutchinson and let him know what's to be done with his son."

Chapter Five

The walk from the parsonage to the sawmill that Josiah's father owned with the Porters was the longest journey Josiah had ever taken.

Thomas Putnam yanked him to a stop once at the whipping post and stocks, which stood not far from the Meeting House. "This is where you shall end up if I have anything to do with it!" he roared at him. He was grasping his arm so tightly that Josiah had lost all feeling in his fingers. "I see that you don't believe me. You think your father is going to save you." He jostled Josiah viciously. "But not this time!"

They marched on and soon came to a halt again when another voice bleated to them from the curve in Ipswich Road.

"You've caught the Hutchinsons at last!" Nathaniel Putnam bellowed as he teetered toward them on his spidery legs.

"Aye!" Thomas and the minister called back in unison.

Not all the Hutchinsons, Josiah thought miserably. *Just the stupid one.* If only they would put him in the stocks and not bring his father into this! Josiah winced, as much from the thought of his father's disappointed eyes as from the vise grip Thomas Putnam still had on his arm.

The cogs of the waterwheel were churning in the river when they finally reached the sawmill, and the blades of the saw they powered were whining so loudly that Thomas Putnam had to shout even louder than he'd already been doing to bring anyone running.

Benjamin Porter emerged first, wiping the sweat from his face with his shirtsleeve and scowling at Thomas Putnam— until he saw Josiah dangling from his hand. He turned at once and hurried back into the square, wooden building that housed the woodcutting mechanism. The blade stopped and silence fell over the Frost Fish River as Joseph Hutchinson tore up the planked walkway with his eyes blazing.

Josiah couldn't watch. He didn't want to see that fiery anger burning into him. That would come soon enough.

"What is the meaning of this?" Papa said.

Thomas Putnam let go of Josiah and pushed him roughly toward his father. "I might ask you the same thing!"

Papa gave Josiah a long look, which Josiah peeked up once to see before quickly returning his eyes to the ground. When his father spoke, it was in a low, even voice. "I warned you once before, Putnam, to never, ever touch one of my children—"

"Even when one of your precious children tries to commit murder on Reverend Parris's family?" There was the edge of a laugh in his voice, and Josiah lifted his head to stare. Thomas Putnam, it seemed, was enjoying this.

"Murder?" Joseph Hutchinson said. "You're mad!"

"Then Reverend Parris is as well," Thomas said. "He's the one who caught him."

Goodman Hutchinson looked at Samuel Parris. "Doing what?"

"Hiding in the bushes at the parsonage while Reverend Parris's child and slaves suffered from his handiwork," Thomas said.

"Why don't you let the man speak for himself?" Papa said. His voice was still quiet, but the warning hung heavily on his tones.

Thomas's broad face simmered, but he bowed with a jerk to Reverend Parris.

"Why, I . . . I thought to go into the Meeting House to pray," Samuel Parris said. "And as I passed by my yard, I saw this . . . this . . . boy crouched in the brush. Moments later, there was a cry from my barn." He blinked furiously, and his voice tottered on the edge of hysteria. "We went to look, and there was my wagon axle, broken in two . . . the wheel on the ground . . . my family hanging on for their lives."

"If by some chance that wagon had gotten out onto the road and then broken," Thomas Putnam put in, "they would all have been dumped out and trampled to death."

"I somehow doubt that, Putnam," Benjamin Porter said. He tried to laugh. "Perhaps a sound tumble to the ground, but certainly not *killed!*"

"This boy didn't know that!" Thomas Putnam shouted. "He had visions of murder when he performed this treachery!"

Papa broke out of his angry calm and shouted, "How do you know what visions he had in his mind?"

And then a new voice was added to the din: "And how do you know it was the boy who did it?"

Everyone turned toward the voice, spoken from farther down the walkway. Josiah caught his breath to keep from gasping out loud. Giles Porter had just stepped out of the mill, and he moved toward them with his smile flashing.

"What are you saying?" Nathaniel Putnam yelped at him. "You weren't there!"

"Nor were you, as far as I can tell," Giles said. He stepped up behind Josiah and put his hand on his shoulder.

Josiah felt himself stiffen. Should he blurt it out right now? Should he tell them he saw Giles coming from Parris's barn and cast all these suspicious eyes on him?

"I would be willing to stake my life on the fact that my son did not take a blade to your wagon axle and set you up for an accident," Papa said, his words back in control.

"And I would be willing to prove it," Giles said. He lifted Josiah's arm. "'Tis a hearty boy, I'll warrant you, but look at this arm—take hold of it if you will."

Thomas started to move toward Josiah's arm, but one look from Papa froze him in his tracks.

"'Twould take a much stronger body than this to do the job you've described, gentlemen," Giles said, letting go of Josiah's arm. His smile burned into the hot air that hung between them. "I doubt young Master Hutchinson here could have held the wagon, sawed into the axle, held the wagon up again to fit the pieces precisely together—"

"Then if he didn't do it," Thomas Putnam said with a screech, "why was he hanging suspiciously about on the parsonage property?"

There was a sudden silence, and Josiah could feel all eyes on him. Thoughts screamed at him from every corner of his mind. *Tell them it was Giles! No, tell them a lie! Tell them—*

"It seems your son has no answer," Nathaniel Putnam said gleefully. "A sure sign of guilt!"

"A sure sign that the boy is frightened nearly out of his wits," Giles said. He patted Josiah's shoulder. "I would guess that young Josiah Hutchinson here was crawling about in Reverend Parris's weeds looking for yarrow. Isn't that what they use to cure snakebite? We all know that was recently a near-tragedy for the Hutchinsons."

There was another silence, this time a confused one. Josiah held his breath. Did anyone in this group know that it was plantain, not yarrow, he would have been looking for? And why was Giles so quick to come to his defense? Josiah stole a look at him. Giles's gray eyes twinkled down at him, and quickly, ever so slightly, he gave Josiah a wink.

"I tell you, this boy is responsible!" Thomas Putnam cried.

"You have no proof, Putnam, and you know it," Joseph Hutchinson said. "I suggest you look elsewhere for your so-called murderer. And while you're at it, I suggest you do some searching inside yourself as well."

Thomas's coal-colored eyes bulged from his head. "Myself? For what reason?"

"To ask yourself why it is so important to you to have my son pay for this crime. 'Tis not about Reverend Parris's safety or even about seeing justice done." Papa moved closer to him and brought a firm finger close to his chest. "'Tis about the Hutchinsons and your never-ending hatred for us. It goes so deeply you would use not only my son, but your own church as a means to vent that hatred." He stepped back and shook his head. "While you're searching, Thomas, look to see if there is any of God left in your heart."

There was an ear-splitting shriek as Thomas Putnam leaped toward Papa. Giles sprang forward and held him back until he stopped struggling. Joseph Hutchinson didn't move at all.

"I suggest you get off our property now, Thomas," Giles said, as if he were talking to a child.

"Let go of me and I shall!" Thomas said. "I've no wish to stay here among murderers and those who would assist them."

Giles chuckled and turned Thomas loose. Putnam shook his jacket as if he had been touched by a dirty pig and stamped off toward the road. His brother Nathaniel scurried after him. Reverend Parris, Josiah noticed, had backed away long before and was retreating up the road as if he were being chased.

Giles looked merrily at Josiah. "You were surely in the wrong place at the wrong time, eh, boy?"

"I'm not sure that we all aren't," Papa said.

They all looked at Joseph Hutchinson. He was leaning on the walkway railing, shoulders sagging as Josiah had seen them do the night of the snakebite.

"What do you mean, Joseph?" Benjamin said.

"Perhaps Salem Village is the wrong place and 1691 the wrong time for good Christians to come together to live brave and decent lives."

"Surely not, Joseph," Giles said. He was still using his soothing voice, and Josiah found his shoulders prickling at the sound of it. "That is why men like your father and Benjamin's came to Massachusetts."

Joseph Hutchinson shook his head. "I think most people here have forgotten those reasons. I think I can no longer live among such people."

"What do you intend to do?" Benjamin Porter said, his voice shaking with alarm.

"The only thing left I have not tried. I want to call a meeting of all the men in this village. Let us sit down prayerfully and see if we can somehow sort out what it is that separates us so and drives us away from God."

Giles gave a hard laugh. "Surely, you can see what bitter fighting that will bring on!"

"Can it be any worse than the fighting that already exists?" Josiah's father said. "Look what happened today. Someone tried to injure the minister and his family!"

Giles shot him one of his smiles. "Now, Joseph, do you not think that with his whining and demands and stiff-necked ways, Reverend Parris brings it on himself?"

"Bodily harm?" Joseph Hutchinson's heavy eyebrows sprang up. "I do not think anyone deserves that, Giles, no matter what the motive, no matter what he may do to 'bring it on himself.' I am shocked that you would even say such a thing."

"Joseph, I didn't mean—"

But Joseph Hutchinson cut off Giles's coaxing words with his own sharp ones. "It seems I never know quite what you mean, Giles. And that grieves me. It grieves me considerably."

The third uncomfortable silence of the afternoon settled over the sawmill walkway. Papa broke it when he looked at

Josiah. "Get you home now. I'm sure you've work to do, and it seems you're strong enough now to do it."

"Aye, sir," Josiah said.

Papa strode down the walkway toward the mill, and Josiah started to go the other way when his eye caught Giles's. The gray Porter eyes looked expectantly at him.

Do you expect me to thank you, Giles? Josiah thought angrily. *If so, I suppose you'll have to wait a long time.*

Josiah turned and, still hobbling, made his way toward home as quickly as possible. The thoughts churned in his head.

Giles saw himself as the hero for saving Josiah from certain hanging at the hands of the Putnams. But it would never occur to him to be honest, to speak up and say it was he who had fixed the wagon so its axle would break. And why would he do such a thing in the first place? Didn't he sit in church like the rest of them every Sunday and hear from the Bible itself—thou shalt not kill? Had God been driven from Giles's heart the way Papa said it had from almost everyone else's?

The questions kept pumping until Josiah rounded the curve in the road, just between the Hutchinsons' house and the parsonage. Everything came to a startled stop as a figure in long, brown skirts dashed across the road toward the Parrises'. Josiah watched in horror as Hope dove for the bushes under Betty Parris's window.

✣ ✣ ✣

Chapter Six

"Hope, no!" Josiah hissed to her as loudly as he dared. Whether she heard him or not, he couldn't tell, for she continued on, headed for certain trouble.

Josiah looked around wildly. Thomas and Nathaniel Putnam were probably hidden somewhere watching them even now. He whipped his head toward the bushes Hope was disappearing behind. Willing his sore leg to move with him, Josiah scrambled forward and threw his arms out to catch her. His fingers caught around her skirts.

"What?" Hope cried out. She whirled to face him, and he gathered more of her skirt into his arms and yanked her out from behind the bushes. She clawed at the ground to hold on.

"What are you doing?" she said in a hoarse whisper.

"Come on," Josiah whispered back. "You can't stay here!"

"Let go of me, you foolish boy!"

"No, it's dangerous here. Come on!"

From the direction of the parsonage, a window creaked open. Josiah's heart started to pound. Wrapping his arms around Hope's legs, he heaved her over his shoulder and stood up. She screamed in his ear, but he wobbled for a moment, pain shooting through his leg, and then limped away.

After several paces, he set her down roughly and grabbed both of her hands in his own, dragging her toward the Hutchinson house. Although she struggled to shake loose, he didn't let go of her until they were inside the woodshed. She sat flat on the ground, fire exploding from her eyes.

"*What* do you think you're doing, Josiah Hutchinson?" she said. Her teeth were clenched together so tightly that the words could barely squeeze out, but Josiah didn't miss the anger in them.

"I had to get you out of there," Josiah said. "And you wouldn't come. You can't go there, Hope."

"You are the one who first took me there!" she cried. "Are you jealous because I am now friends with Betty Parris, too?"

"No! Reverend Parris knows about the spot. And the Putnams."

Her eyes narrowed. "How?"

"Because . . . because Reverend Parris caught me there today."

Hope rolled her eyes and snatched up her skirts. "That's just fine, Josiah. Why couldn't you be careful? Now there is no way I can—"

"They accused me of trying to murder Reverend Parris and his family!" Josiah said.

Hope sank into her skirt again. "What?"

"I was hiding there, hoping to talk to Betty, when

Reverend Parris pulled me out. Right then, we heard scream-ing from the barn. When we got there, someone had tampered with the axle, and it had broken. Everyone was holding on to the wagon—except Abigail." Josiah couldn't resist a snort. "She was lying among the horse dung."

"And they accused you of doing it?" Hope said.

"Aye. Dragged me to the sawmill and told Papa I was a murderer. Only because Giles Porter stepped in did they leave me alone. But he—"

Josiah stopped. After the last time he and Hope had talked about Giles, was she ready to hear this?

"That's wretched," Hope said. Then she sighed. "Of course we can't get to Betty that way now, but I need her. I need her to send a message for me."

Her chin drooped, something Josiah had almost never seen it do. He sat down carefully beside her.

"What's so important?" he said.

She shrugged vaguely as she studied the tops of her shoes. "I can't tell you."

"But what if you get into trouble and I don't know what's going on? How can I get you out of it?"

Hope knitted her eyebrows together as she looked at him. "Get me out of it?"

"Aye. Isn't that what we always do—look out for each other?"

"I suppose," she said.

"Think back to last summer when they accused you of stealing that gold chain, and I proved you didn't. And last winter when you were always there to keep Papa from asking me questions I didn't want to answer."

Slowly, Hope nodded. "We do stand up for each other, I guess."

"Sometimes we're the only ones who will," Josiah said. He kicked at a piece of stray bark and stole a sideways look at her. "So maybe I can help you now. I know how to deliver messages, too."

Hope was quiet for a long time before she puffed up her chest with air.

She's getting ready to tell me something big, Josiah thought.

"All right," she said finally. "But you must promise not to tell anyone—and you have to promise that you won't try to talk me out of it. I know what I'm doing." To prove it, she tilted her chin up and tossed her dark curls back. The look she shot Josiah dared him to disagree.

"All right, I promise," Josiah said. He leaned forward, and his skin tingled. This was important, and she was finally letting him in on it.

"For the last few weeks," she began, "I have been stealing away to Edward Putnam's farm when I can, as you already know."

Josiah nodded.

"What you don't know is why." She took another deep breath. "When Jonathon and Richard and Eleazer Putnam were all taken off to the stocks for what they . . . for what they tried to do to me last spring, Silas came out to the flax field one day when I was harvesting it by myself. He wanted to tell me he was sorry for what his cousins did, even though he wasn't part of it. We talked and I found out that he's . . . he's different from the other Putnams." She nibbled gently at her lip.

"Different how?" Josiah said. He could hear warning thoughts whispering at the edges of his brain.

"He's quiet, and he's not rough and stupid. I think he's a good person deep down, especially when he isn't with . . . them." She thought for a minute, and then she turned to face Josiah head on. "I might as well just say it," she said firmly. "I like him."

"You like Silas Putnam?"

"Aye. And he invited me to come to his farm whenever he was working . . . to watch."

Josiah curled his lip. "Watch what?"

"Watch *him*."

Josiah stared at his sister in amazement. It looked for all the world as if she were watching Silas now, the way her eyes shined and the color fluffed up into her cheeks like a sunrise.

Josiah shook his head. This made no sense. He needed to go back a little. "You agreed to be friends with a cousin of Jonathon Putnam's?" he said.

"Yes," Hope said crisply. She was ready for him. "Just as you agreed to be friends with a cousin of Abigail Williams's— or a half brother of Thomas Putnam's." She looked at him with a determined expression. "There is no difference, Josiah Hutchinson."

"But you can't go out there to Edward Putnam's farm anymore!" Josiah said. "Just as I can't go to the bushes on the Parrises' land to meet Betty. I saw Silas's father. He almost caught you there."

Hope nodded. "I know. That's why I need Betty—to take a message to Silas. We have to arrange some other way to meet."

Josiah shot up like a ball from a musket and stared down

on her. "You are out of your mind! You call me brainless and foolish, but this is just mad! You know the rules—girls are not allowed to meet with boys alone! You might as well throw yourself to the bears!"

Hope stood up, too, and met her brother nose to nose. "I knew it!" she shouted into his face. "I knew I couldn't expect anyone to understand—including you. *Especially* you!"

"I don't understand anyone who does something danger-ous—for no reason!"

"There is a reason," she said tightly. "And that's just what you don't understand."

As she bolted from the woodshed and left the door swing-ing behind her, Josiah had to admit she was right. He didn't understand.

It was hot inside the Hutchinsons' house after supper that night, and Mama and Hope went outside to sit on the step to stitch, talk, and enjoy any evening breezes that hap-pened to wisp their way. Josiah hung around awkwardly and tried to catch a few fireflies, but everything seemed restless and pointless.

Hope wouldn't even look at him, and the questions in his head wouldn't leave him alone. Perhaps, he decided, it was time to go to the one place where he could always figure things out.

It was only a short walk to the spot on Hathorne's Hill that overlooked Thomas Putnam's farm on one side and Wolf Pits Meadow on the other. He could still remember the first time his father had brought him here and told him it was called the Blessing Place—the very place where Josiah's grandfather, Joseph Hutchinson Sr., had stood when he had first come to Salem Village and asked for God's blessings on his family and all he owned.

Tonight, Josiah was happy to see that summer grass and wildflowers nearly covered the charred ground left when the old shack that once stood here had burned down. That fire brought back unhappy memories, but the place, the Blessing Place, always brought him peace.

He had barely settled into a spot against a smooth rock and plucked a dandelion to chew on when he heard footfalls approaching from the other side of the hill. Was there never any place to be alone? His breath quickened. And was there any place safe from the Putnams? This was Hutchinson land, stuck in the middle of Putnam holdings, but the Putnams tended to have short memories. Josiah's breathing came even faster. Hadn't the Putnam cousins been released just a few days ago—the day of the snakebite?

He flung the dandelion stem aside and got to his feet, but a deep voice from behind stopped him.

"Josiah, is that you?" his father said. Josiah turned in surprise. Papa? Up here? Wandering around aimlessly the way Josiah did, instead of home reading a book and bettering himself?

"Will you share the Blessing Place with me tonight?" his father said.

"Aye, sir," Josiah said quickly.

Papa motioned for him to sit again and took a seat on a nearby rock. He plucked a dandelion and, to Josiah's amazement, stuck the stem between his teeth just the way Josiah and his friends did.

"I see you've much to occupy your thoughts tonight, too," Papa said. "And have you come here to make decisions?"

Josiah felt his heart trip over a beat.

"That is why I've come," Joseph Hutchinson went on. "I'd forgotten that the Blessing Place is a perfect place for such things on a summer evening—until I saw you headed this way."

Josiah didn't know what to say, so he nodded and listened. As Papa talked, Josiah could almost see his father's thoughts being tossed into piles, as if he were sorting them out, and more for himself than for Josiah.

"Everyone is a sinner, Josiah," he said. "But anyone who is born anew enters into a covenant of grace, a binding agreement with God, that says if he repents of those sins, he will live in everlasting life with the Lord." He shook his head sadly. "My father, Benjamin's father, Thomas Putnam's father—they all believed that an entire nation could enter into such a covenant. They thought we were all chosen by God to come to this new continent and live godly lives like visible saints. That is what I have tried to do, did you know that?"

Josiah nodded silently.

"I have tried to make my decisions for the honor, service, and glory of God. And every step of the way, the Putnams have accused me of doing the work of the Lord deceitfully. Do you understand why, Josiah?"

Josiah shook his head, but his heart quickened. He had always wanted to know, and maybe now the mystery would at last be solved.

"Because I believe that whatever gifts God gives me I should use to His glory, and His glory includes providing for my family, giving to the poor, and improving the community I have come to cherish."

A warmth had come into his father's voice that Josiah could feel burning his own face. It was a fire of passion, and it flashed in his father's eyes as he spoke.

"So I chose to become a partner in the Porters' sawmill," Papa went on. "And I chose to trade with Phillip English and build up a business for the Hutchinsons. The farm is for our own survival, but limiting ourselves to it is like wasting God's gifts." He laughed softly. "The Putnams would have you believe that I am greedy, selfish, and interested only in earthly possessions. I cannot judge them, but they might do well to turn that accusation on themselves—and on Reverend Parris. I do not think any of them bad men, especially the minister. He answered God's call, so there must be good in him. But I do think them somewhat misguided by jealousy. They need to spend some time at the Blessing Place, eh?"

"Aye," Josiah said.

"But I am the one here making decisions tonight, as are you."

It grew quiet on the hillside, but not in Josiah's mind. Questions begged to be spoken. He looked at his father, who searched the sun with tired eyes, lines deepening on his face. Josiah thought perhaps he shouldn't ask any, but how else could he possibly find out? How else could he know what to do, about Hope, about anything?

"Papa?" he said timidly.

"Aye. Speak up."

Josiah formed his words carefully. "How do you make your decisions?"

"With much difficulty, I'm afraid," his father said. "For you see, the answers are seldom black and white. You have to find the right shade of gray in God's will."

Josiah sighed. He had been hearing about God's will since he was old enough to sit on his mother's lap in the Meeting House. Everyone else seemed to always know what that was and talked of it as if they had heard it spoken by Him at their supper table. "'Tis God's will," everyone said so easily when someone died or someone's house burned down.

Josiah looked carefully at his father, who seemed to be waiting.

"How do you know what God's will is?" Josiah said.

"You gather as much information as you can," Papa said. "From the Bible, of course. From wise people around you. From your experiences. You take in these things the way we harvest the grain in the autumn, eh? And when these things you've collected come together in the right way, you feel a peace." He pointed toward the darkening summer sky. "'Tis like that gray mist that covers the village before the sun goes down. We feel at peace as night comes, do we not?"

Josiah looked at the last of the day's sunlight and nodded.

"So I must follow that same course now," Papa said. His voice hardened, as if it were time to stop talking and take action. "I must gather more information, listen to the other side. I'm afraid I have heard too much Porter of late."

He didn't say any more but continued to look off into the sky that now grew darker and darker.

Josiah settled into the quiet with his own thoughts. "Gather information," Papa had said. Maybe that's what he should do, and perhaps that was what Hope was trying to do.

Could she make a decision about being friends with Silas without knowing more than that he was hateful Jonathon Putnam's cousin?

Not according to Papa, Josiah decided.

He lay back on the new grass and listened to his father's even breathing as he struggled with his own choices. All right, then. He would help her. The only question was how.

Chapter Seven

The next morning at breakfast, Josiah's father was all business again. The peaceful glow of their hillside conversation had been replaced by the need to keep the farm running.

"Josiah," he said as he pushed his chair back from the breakfast table, "you and your sister will harvest that swamp grass for the cattle today. 'Tis high enough now. I noticed it yesterday."

Josiah saw Hope pull her napkin in front of her mouth to hide her curling lip. But she wasn't fast enough for Papa.

"This task doesn't please you, Hope?" he said, his blue eyes piercing her.

"No, sir," she stammered. "I mean . . . "

Papa looked back and forth between Hope and Josiah. "Would you rather be Edward Putnam's children?"

Hope's eyes widened to the size of her wooden plate, and Josiah choked on his bread.

"He has his son and his nephews digging ditches for him this week."

"Ditches?" Mama said. "For what?"

"To mark his property boundaries," Papa said grimly. "As if he and all the other Putnams didn't constantly announce their ownings to all of us on every possible occasion." He turned his riveting gaze on Hope again. "So would you rather work at ditches or swing a scythe a few times?"

"I shall harvest the swamp grass, Papa," Hope said in a tiny voice. "And I shall do it with grace."

"Good, then." Papa stood up and dropped his napkin next to his pewter trencher. "Go now, before that wretched heat begins to bear down on us. 'Tis the hottest summer I can ever remember in Massachusetts."

As soon as the breakfast dishes were washed and put away and Mama was supplied with enough firewood for the rest of the morning's housework, Hope and Josiah took two curved scythes from their nails on the barn wall and headed for the only patch of marshy ground on the Hutchinsons' land. Joseph Hutchinson made good use of even this otherwise worthless piece of property, and he had sent Josiah out in the spring to plant grass seed there. As Hope and Josiah reached the swampy area, Josiah could see that it had grown almost to their knees. Once it was cut, it would be taken back and fed to the cattle.

That's what Papa means by using the gifts God has given you, Josiah thought. But as soon as they started to work, his thoughts turned to the matter at hand.

Next to him, Hope swung her blade viciously. *She wishes that were my head she was chopping off*, Josiah decided. He would have to be careful how he spoke.

"So, what is it you want to do?" he said finally. "With Silas, I mean."

She left her scythe in midair. "What do you care?" she said. "You already told me I was crazy."

"Perhaps I've changed my mind," Josiah said. "But I just need to know—what is it you want?"

Hope lowered the blade and searched his face before she answered. "I just want to find out if he's as good a person as he seems to be, away from his cousins," she said. Her voice was guarded, but Josiah could see the hint of a glow in her eyes. "I have to do it secretly, though, until I can convince Mama and Papa that he is good."

"So you're just trying to gather information to make a decision," Josiah said.

Her eyes leaped to meet his. "Well, yes, that's exactly right." She shrugged suddenly. "But you don't understand that, so why are we talking about it?"

"I *do* understand it," Josiah said. "I mean, I understand that you want to, I just don't know *why* you want to. But maybe that's the part that's none of my business."

A smile spread slowly over Hope's face. "You'll help me, then?" she said.

"Aye. Well, I, uh . . . " Josiah cleared his throat and pretended to study the swamp for just the right clump of grass to attack next. There was one thing that still bothered him, and he knew she was going to blow up like a kitchen fire if he wasn't careful how he asked about it.

"Well?" Hope said.

Josiah didn't look at her. "I have to know one thing,

because I will never help anyone do anything . . . that isn't . . . you know . . . "

"What is it?" she said impatiently. "Sometimes you are so maddening, Josiah!"

"I need to know—" Josiah could feel his face going scarlet, and he began to chop savagely at the swamp grass. "You and Silas, you're not going to . . . kiss or anything, are you?"

"Josiah Hutchinson!" Hope cried. "How could you ask such a thing?"

"Well, are you?"

"Certainly not! Whatever made you think—?"

"You were talking the other day about husbands and getting married and—"

"I am not interested in marrying Silas Putnam!" Hope said. "Or anyone else! But I'm 14. I need to know about what it is that makes men . . . so . . . so different. And Silas is the one I want to know it about."

Josiah frowned. "Then you won't be committing a sin, or breaking your covenant, I mean, with God?"

"Not unless God wants us to continue hating other people for no reason," she said fiercely.

Josiah nodded slowly.

"Then you'll help me?" she said.

It was the closest he had ever heard her come to begging, and for a minute he wanted to draw it out just a little more. But he knew Hope. Too much teasing and he could forget the whole thing.

"All right, then," he said. "I'll talk to Silas."

Hope squealed and dropped her scythe. She looked as if she were going to throw her arms around him, and Josiah put up his hands in front of him.

"We have to do it my way," he said quickly.

"What is your plan?" she said.

"First, I have to get to Silas, and I think I know how. Didn't Papa say he'd be digging ditches for his father to mark their property?"

"Aye."

"Tomorrow morning—early—I'll go there before my own chores and see if I can catch him. It's the only way I can think of."

"And it's a good way. I know it is!" Hope said. Shiny tears had come to her eyes and again she threw her arms out. This time he wasn't quick enough, and she caught Josiah in a hug. He wriggled away, cheeks burning.

"No following me," he said sternly. "I'll arrange a safe meeting place for you where no one will see."

"Aye, I'll leave it all to you." She stood looking at him, eyes sparkling, face rosy. Josiah bent over his scythe and squirmed inside his shirt.

"You're a fine brother, Josiah," she said.

"Ach," he said.

"Josiah!" a voice whispered to him the next morning.

Josiah opened his eyes and blinked into the darkness.

"If you go now, you can be gone before Papa wakes up," Hope said.

Josiah turned over and moaned. "Go where?" he said sleepily.

"To see Silas. Don't you remember?"

Josiah sat up on his cot. It was still completely dark in the room. Through the diamond-shaped panes of their window, he could see stars sparkling in the sky.

"Are you sure it's morning?" he said.

"It will be soon enough," she said. "Please, Josiah, go now so there will be no trouble."

Josiah tried to shake the cobwebs out of his head. When he stood up, Hope already had his shirt and breeches waiting for him.

"I shall put your boots by the front door while you get dressed," she said.

He was surprised she didn't offer to dress him. He wanted to remind her that Silas wouldn't be out digging ditches before the sun came up, but he knew it would do no good. Still rubbing the sleep from his eyes, he got dressed and padded silently down the steps.

Hope was waiting with his boots by the door.

"I want to say something to you, Josiah," she said as he laced the boots onto his feet. "This is important to me, but don't put yourself in any danger at all. Don't allow yourself to be caught by the other Putnams."

Josiah squinted up at her. "I thought you said they wouldn't dare touch us now."

"Aye, and I'm sure they won't. But just in case."

"You needn't worry, because they're never going to see me," Josiah said. He stood up and quietly pulled open the front door. "I'll come back with news."

Even though the sheen in her eyes and the arm she flung around his neck made him twitch and hurry to get out, he did feel a little like a hero. He was putting himself in some danger—perhaps just a little—so his sister could have something she wanted. That was brave, he had to admit.

He rounded the corner of the house, and then his heart stood still. There was something there—there in the early morning shadow of the oak tree. Josiah sucked in his breath and leaned against the side of the house. Slowly, almost gracefully, it moved, until two large, soft, brown eyes were looking right into his. The ears perked up, and then just as gently it glided off into the darkness.

Josiah closed his eyes. He was glad no one had seen him nearly die of fright over a deer. All right, so perhaps he wasn't all that brave.

He made his way easily up the Ipswich River, and as he crept quietly among the rocks and rushes, the world began to wake up. He could hear a rooster crowing on Thomas Putnam's farm, and as he neared Edward Putnam's land, a few cows greeted him with sleepy moos as he passed their pasture. There wasn't much there for them to eat for breakfast, Josiah noticed. He couldn't see why Edward was so anxious for people to know which property was his. Josiah wouldn't have given a shilling for any of it himself.

Approaching the swampland where he had first seen Hope with Silas, Josiah slowed down and kept his eyes to the ground. Just after dawn was a favorite time for snakes to come out for breakfast, too. Josiah shuddered as he pictured the old snake's diamond head reared back with fangs bared at him. He, Ezekiel, and William had always played with green snakes in summer, but now he wasn't sure he could even look one of those in the eye anymore.

Once he got to the edge of Edward Putnam's farm, Josiah

thought he would be in for a long wait, so he found a large rock on a tiny patch of dry land to hide behind while he bided his time. He pulled up his whistle pouch on his leg so it wouldn't dangle into sight, and he noticed for the first time that it was bulkier than usual.

Warily, he peeked in, and then smiled. There was a piece of bread inside, folded in so the butter wouldn't get on the cloth. Hope. She had seen him devour enough breakfasts at dawn to know he would be hungry.

He had barely pulled the bread out of the pouch when he heard voices from the Putnam farm. He crouched down as low as he could and peeked around the rock. There, coming from the house with shovels in hand were Silas and Eleazer Putnam.

Silas marched straight to the edge of the property—the imaginary line everyone already knew about—and poked his shovel into the dirt.

"We start here," Silas said. "Get digging before the heat starts."

Eleazer slunk down onto a rock and leaned on his shovel. "In time," he said. "Do you know I've not even had breakfast yet?"

"Dig a while and Papa will bring us some bread," Silas said. He had already dug his shovel into the ground three times.

"Bread!" Eleazer cried in disbelief. "They gave us better than that at the Salem Town jail!"

"Only because your father and Reverend Parris paid for it," Silas said.

Josiah had to clap his hand over his mouth to keep from

gasping. Reverend Parris had paid for the meals of three criminals?

"Come on, Eleazer," Silas said testily. "Get you to digging."

"I'm barely awake yet. Give me leave a while." Eleazer let his shovel drop to the ground and stretched out over a rock. The sun was just beginning to peek over the farmhouse, and Eleazer turned his face toward it like a drowsy cat. "I shall dig as soon as I've had my sleep."

Josiah watched as Eleazer wiggled around for a minute and then closed his eyes. Within a minute, his mouth had fallen open, and a trail of drool was seeping from its corner. Josiah smiled to himself. This was going to be easier than he could have dreamed. He waited until a few snorts and snuffles puffed out of Eleazer's nose before he tiptoed from behind the rock and inched his way toward Silas.

Silas was hard at his digging, grunting and already sweating even in the dewy coolness of morning.

I'll get to that next rock, the one right beside him, Josiah thought, *and beckon him to join me behind it.*

Not making a sound, Josiah made his way to the rock and sank behind it. He listened. Eleazer was still breathing like a thunderstorm. The shovel made several more dips into the ground, and then it stopped. Silas would be taking a moment to wipe the sweat off his forehead. Now was the time to move, before Edward Putnam came out with their breakfast.

Josiah rose slowly and steadily until his eyes were just over the top of the rock. Silas had his back to him.

"Psst!" Josiah hissed softly.

It wasn't a harsh sound. Josiah was sure Silas could barely have heard it. But Silas jumped and whirled around, and his shovel left his hand and fell over. The handle hit squarely in the middle of Eleazer's sleeping face.

Eleazer started awake and yelled. Silas whipped his head from his cousin to Josiah and back again. Josiah didn't wait for him to do it again. He was tearing back down to the river before Eleazer could even get himself off the rock.

"Who was that? Was that Hutchinson?" Eleazer shouted. There was no answer from Silas that Josiah could hear. He only knew there were footsteps pounding after him. He didn't have to look over his shoulder to know they were Eleazer's. The boy never stopped screaming insults as he tore after him.

"Stupid, brainless fool!" Eleazer cried. "What were you about on my uncle's property? Come back here!"

Josiah, of course, did not stop, but pumped as hard as he could toward the river, dodging tree branches and rocks as he went. He figured he could outrun Eleazer. He was Josiah's age, but like all the Putnams, he was skinny and lanky and didn't have Josiah's stocky strength. But if he didn't get rid of him soon, Jonathon and Richard were sure to show up—if not Silas, too. The Putnams seemed to have instincts for when one of them was entangled with a Hutchinson, Proctor, or Porter.

The river came into view. He could dive in and swim for safety, since he could swim and Eleazer couldn't. But then he would have to go home soaked and explain that to Mama and Papa. And then an idea popped into Josiah's head. This was going to be much better.

Eleazer was still screaming as they approached the bank, and Josiah slowed his pace. His heart started to hammer as he let Eleazer get close, but he slowed even more, until he could almost feel young Putnam's hot breath on the back of his neck.

"Ha! I've got you!" Eleazer cried.

Josiah could see his hands out of the corner of his eye, reaching around to grab him. Josiah dug his feet into the ground and tucked down into a ball. Eleazer flew right over his head, straight into the river.

The water was only a few feet deep at the edge, Josiah knew, but Eleazer splashed and sputtered as if he were drowning in the middle of the ocean.

Of course, he might be drowning, Josiah thought suddenly. *I can't leave him here to die.*

Josiah was about to strip off his shirt and go in after him, perhaps making Eleazer promise to leave him alone if he saved him, when he heard more footsteps coming from behind.

"Eleazer?" said Silas.

"Help me! Save me, Silas!" Eleazer shouted shamelessly.

Josiah could hear the tears in his voice, and he smiled to himself. Quickly, he darted away, down the riverbank, and hid behind a row of bulrush. Silas appeared, and Eleazer continued to scream.

"He pushed me in the river! He tried to drown me!"

"You fell in yourself because you're a clumsy ox," Silas said as Josiah watched him pick up a branch and poke it toward his cousin. "No Hutchinson would try to kill someone, so shut it. Here, grab on to this."

Eleazer flailed his arms around and finally snagged the branch. Silas pulled him to the shore and turned around to walk away.

"I shall tell on him!" Eleazer cried.

"If you do, I shall tell my father that you refused to help me dig the ditches."

"Why are you protecting those . . . those Hutchinsons?" Eleazer sputtered as he dragged himself from the ground and followed his cousin.

Silas didn't answer. And Josiah was pretty sure he knew why.

Chapter Eight

Josiah went straight from the river to his work. He didn't see Hope until he came in for breakfast with a basket of eggs. She followed his every move with eyes full of questions.

"You're out and about early," Papa commented.

"Aye, sir."

"You'll have a successful place of your own someday if the Lord is willing and you continue to work this hard."

"Aye, sir," Josiah said again.

He turned guiltily to his trencher of corn mush and molasses, avoiding Hope's eyes. Although Papa didn't say so directly, Josiah knew his father was proud of him. Would he be so proud if he knew Josiah was sneaking around, trying to connect Hope with a Putnam—no matter what the reason? Perhaps he should just tell Hope he had tried and it wasn't going to work.

"Hope," Papa said suddenly.

Josiah nearly came out of his chair. Had Papa read his mind?

"Your mother will need extra help from you today."

"Aye, sir," Hope said. She had no trouble looking right into his eyes, Josiah noticed, even when she had everything to hide.

"There is to be a meeting right after dinner of as many of the village church members as will come—right here in this kitchen. There is much to be done to set it to rights."

"'Tis a good help, this one," Mama said. She smoothed a hand over Hope's black curls. "You've naught to worry. She always lightens my load."

Josiah studied his porridge and tried to swallow a lump of it that had lodged in his throat. Both of their parents trusted them. Was it ever right to go behind their backs, even if it were just to "gather information"?

He felt a poke at his shin, and he looked up. Hope was staring at him from across the table.

"Perhaps Josiah could help me air the table linens," she said, eyes looking right at Josiah and sparkling.

He moaned inwardly. She was setting it up so he would have to tell her what happened—and what he planned to do next.

"It's sure you can air the linens yourself, Hope," Papa said. "I've another job for your brother."

Hope's eyes turned stony, but Josiah tried to cover his relief as he said, "What would you have me do, sir?"

"Go you to John Proctor's. He has not been coming to church much of late, and I want to be sure he has gotten the word that there is to be a meeting here tonight."

"Is John so angry with the church that he would risk punishment again by not attending services?" Mama asked.

"Aye, and that is exactly why it is so important for him to be here tonight. We may be able to settle some of those quarrels that keep him away."

Josiah rose hurriedly from the table and practically ran for the door. "I shall be on my way to the Proctors at once," he said. He didn't have to look over his shoulder to know that Hope's eyes were boring in on him.

The Proctors lived some distance from the Hutchinsons, on the other side of Felton's Hill just off Ipswich Road. Like Josiah's father, William Proctor's papa had another business besides his farm. He ran an inn for travelers coming in and out of the village. William and his sister, Sarah, could always find out helpful pieces of information by listening in on the conversations that were held there.

But nothing they could pick up was going to help Josiah this time, he decided as he ran through the long grass and wildflowers toward the Proctors'. *I'm going to have to figure my own way out of my deal with Hope.*

As he climbed onto the rock wall that bordered the Proctor farm, Josiah fumbled in his pouch between the tiny knife and the flint, took out a wooden whistle, and blew a signal. William met him before he got halfway to the house.

"Josiah!" he said, his face beaming under the almost-white spikes of hair that both he and his sister, Sarah, had inherited from their father. "How is it you've gotten away from your work?" He sneaked a glance toward his house. "I may never see anything but the dirt of this farm again. My father has me workin' every minute. And we work even harder when his mind's in a tangle about something, like it is now."

Josiah nodded sympathetically. His own father was a task-master, but John Proctor was known for the burdensome work he expected out of the people under him, including his son.

"Is he coming to the meeting tonight?" Josiah said. "Perhaps he can get untangled there, eh?"

Suddenly, a gravelly voice interrupted. "Aye, I'll be there." Both Josiah and William jumped.

John Proctor strode out of the barn and toward the boys. His craggy, square face was somber with trouble and sweat.

"Have you come from your father?" Mr. Proctor said.

"Aye, sir."

"Then you tell him I shall be there to support him." He took off his broad-rimmed beaver hat and wiped his dripping face with his sleeve. "But I have very little faith that this meeting is going to change anything, not with the Putnams there. The only way to have the look of peace is to run them out of town or become their friends. I'm unwilling to do either."

Neither William nor Josiah said a word, but Josiah knew John Proctor wasn't expecting a reply. Goodman Proctor fixed his hat back onto his straw-colored hair and looked at William.

"You finish mending that wall yonder, and I'll give you leave to come with me to the Hutchinsons' tonight. Sarah, too. You'll need friends like them someday—just as I have."

He turned quickly away, and just as quickly William made a move to follow him. Too much dawdling and John Proctor might change his mind. But as he went, William gave Josiah a wide grin. Josiah flashed him an even wider one. With William and Sarah around, he wouldn't have to answer any questions from Hope. And maybe by tomorrow, she would forget all about Silas Putnam.

The afternoon passed quickly, what with tending the animals, gathering wood, and giving Hope the slip. Every time Josiah passed the kitchen window, she leaned out and hissed to him, but he pretended not to hear.

Once right after dinner when he went out to give the vegetable leavings to the pigs, Hope hiked up her skirts and started to run after him, but the Proctors' wagon pulled in front of the house and Sarah Proctor called to her from across the yard.

Hope stood for a minute, looking first at Josiah, then back at Sarah. Josiah took that opportunity to dart for the pigpen. Pigs usually didn't get you into corners and ask you questions.

As the men of Salem Village began to arrive, William joined Josiah on the fence to watch. They could see Hope and Sarah inside, pouring the cider into pitchers and piling corn cakes and blackberry tarts onto trays.

"I wonder if there will be any of those left for us," William said as he craned his neck to see.

Josiah grunted. "Just as long as Hope isn't the one to come serving it to us," he said.

"I don't care who serves it to us. Your mother makes the best tarts in Essex County. I'd let Ann Putnam Jr. bring me one!"

Josiah cocked his head. "Would you, William?" he said. "I mean, truly?"

"I was only foolin'!" William said. "I'd eat dirt before I'd take a scrap from any of the Putnams—except Joseph, of course."

"Even if you found out that one of them wasn't so bad? That he could be trusted?"

It was William's turn to grunt. "That will happen when pigs sprout wings and fly!" he said.

William stretched himself tall on the fence again and spied toward the window. Josiah's gaze followed, but he didn't see the mound of tarts and cakes.

What he saw through the flung-open windows of the Hutchinson kitchen was like a painting. There on one side of it were the Putnams, posed with their big, red-skinned heads and narrow shoulders, arms crossing their chests, lips pursed like they had all eaten onion tarts instead of blackberry. With them was Reverend Parris, whose narrow eyes moved as anxiously as his fingers did around and around the handkerchief he clutched.

On the other side of the "painting" were the Porters, Joseph Putnam, John Proctor, the Houltons, the Nurses, the Cloyces, and the Jacobs. They were all crouched forward in their chairs, brows furrowed in concern, eyes searching each others' faces, hands twisting nervously on the tabletop in front of them.

Between the two knots of Salem Villagers stood Josiah's father, his big, rough hands pressed on the table, his piercing blue eyes penetrating every face, the lines in his own face working hard to convince them.

Occasionally, a sentence his father spoke would waft from the window:

"We may have our differences, but we all serve the same God. Can we not start there?"

"Mr. Parris, you are a minister of the Lord, and we must

all respect that, but we must also know that what you do is for the Lord and not some other master."

"Times are changing, and we must change with them. We can do that with decency if we remember that it is only God who never changes."

"I think we must pray together over the future of our church community—not bicker in our little clans over money and property and power."

It was a picture of his father trying to bring the enemies together, Josiah knew. Papa was looking right at Thomas, Nathaniel, John, and Edward Putnam as he spoke.

John Proctor had said one of the two ways to have peace was to become friends with the Putnams. But he didn't say all of them. Maybe just one Putnam would do. Could Josiah and Hope perhaps help their father by getting Silas Putnam on their side? Wouldn't that show the grown-ups that what their father was trying to do could actually be done?

Josiah grabbed William's arm. "It's time for the Merry Band to go to work," he said.

William's wide, blue eyes grew even wider. "The Merry Band? You mean . . . against the Putnams?"

"Nay," Josiah said, yanking William off the fence and guiding him down the road. "For the Putnams!"

William badgered him with questions all the way to the Porters' farm, but Josiah said he wouldn't answer any of them until they were with Ezekiel. Then he would reveal his plan to both of them.

They found Ezekiel sitting on his front step scraping a knife across a piece of flint. He stuffed both items into his pouch when he saw his two friends tearing across the yard.

"I thought I'd go out of my skull, I'm so bored!" he said. "What say you to a wade in the river?"

"We can go to the river," Josiah said. "But we've no time to play. We need to have a meeting."

Both boys were ready to jump out of their skins when Josiah finally settled on the rocks at the edge of the Frost Fish River and told his and Hope's story. William's eyes grew so wide that Josiah was sure they would pop out of his head. Ezekiel, looking skeptical, closed his wide-set gray eyes into slits.

"She's gone mad," Ezekiel said flatly when Josiah was finished. "If Rachel ever looked at a Putnam, my father would have her at the whipping post, and then Giles would take a turn at her."

"Aye," William said. He shuddered as if he were picturing his father, John Proctor, chasing after Sarah.

"Your fathers aren't my father," Josiah said. "My papa wants to see the quarrels between the Putnams and us settled, because that's God's will. If there's some good in Silas Putnam, perhaps Hope can help by being friends with him."

"Or she can fall into their trap," Ezekiel said. He shifted his weight against the rocks and leaned back against a poplar, propping his hands behind his head. William was watching him anxiously.

"What trap?" Josiah said.

"The one the Putnams are setting for her, the one Silas is luring her into by pretending to be a saint among devils." He nudged William, who was still looking at him. "You know they want to get back at us for what happened last spring."

"Or Silas sees that we aren't foolin' anymore, and they won't get away with their threats now," Josiah said.

Ezekiel hooted. "You *are* foolin' if you think that! Giles says the Putnams—"

"I don't care what Giles says!" Josiah cried. "I care what my father says. We have to gather information. Hope can do that if we help her."

"We?" Ezekiel said. "Don't count us into your little plan. We're brave, but we're not stupid, eh, William?"

William didn't answer but knitted his brows in the direction of his toes.

"William?" Ezekiel said.

"What?" William snapped at him.

"You agree with me, don't you? We tangled with the Putnams and finally got them punished. We're not going to chance it again, right?"

"Maybe you aren't," William said, squirming under Ezekiel's gaze. "But I wish you'd let me speak for myself."

Ezekiel pulled back his chin in surprise. "Go on, then. Speak. But you're as daft as he is if you go along with it."

"We don't even know what it is he wants us to do yet," William said. His voice was a little trembly, but Josiah looked at him with admiration. A year ago, William would never have thought of standing up to Ezekiel.

"All right, then," Ezekiel said. He sat up and put his hands on his skinny hips. "What's your plan, Josiah?"

"Well, I don't quite have a complete plan yet," Josiah said slowly. Ezekiel started to laugh, but Josiah cut him off. "We've always planned *together*. I thought I could depend on you to help me—both of you."

"I'll help you," William said softly. Josiah and Ezekiel looked at him. He hitched up his shoulders inside his shirt, but he looked right back at Ezekiel. "You didn't see those men in Josiah's kitchen, Ezekiel," he said. "They're trying to make things right again. Why shouldn't we?"

Josiah thought William had seen only the refreshments. He grinned proudly at his friend and then shifted his eyes to Ezekiel.

Ezekiel was gnawing on a fingernail and staring down the river. "Well, if I don't help you," he said finally, "you're sure to get yourselves into some kind of trouble you can't get out of without me."

"Ha!" William cried. "Who needs you, Ezekiel Porter! You—"

"You're right, Ezekiel," Josiah interrupted. "We do need you. So let's get started."

Ezekiel's eyes took on the excited gleam they always got when there were plans to be made. "It's nearly dark. I'd best make a fire for us to see by." He pulled out his knife and flint and began to scrape.

William got some sticks together, and Josiah breathed a sigh of relief. He didn't care how much pride he'd had to swallow to get Ezekiel to help them. They were all in it together now, and that was what mattered. He hoped things were going as well back in his kitchen.

Josiah was even more grateful for their help when, in the murky gray of dawn the next day, the three stationed themselves at the edge of Edward Putnam's property and saw not only Silas and Eleazer Putnam stalk sleepily toward their unfinished ditch, but Richard Putnam, too.

"I thought you said—" Ezekiel started to hiss in Josiah's ear.

But Josiah shook his head and watched. On his other side, he could feel William tightening with fear.

"Get you away from me!" Silas barked at his cousins.

Eleazer, who had been at his elbow, backed away. When Silas turned his head, Eleazer stuck out his tongue at him.

Ezekiel smothered a laugh with his hand, and Josiah gave him a poke. This would work only if they could get Silas away from his cousins. But if either Richard or Eleazer found them . . .

"Now?" Ezekiel whispered.

Eleazer had followed his older cousin Richard about 20 paces to one end of the ditch and reluctantly stuck his shovel into the dirt. Richard lifted one small pile and leaned on his shovel to rest, his head turned away.

"Now," Josiah agreed.

As soundlessly as cats, William and Ezekiel left Josiah's side and slipped toward Richard and Eleazer's end of the ditch. Josiah waited until he heard the first whistle and then the second before he moved toward Silas's end.

"What was that?" Eleazer said.

"Something to keep you from working," Silas said. "Now shut it and keep digging."

"No, I heard it, too!" Richard said.

They all froze like Puritan statues, and the two whistles came again.

"D'ya think 'tis Indians?" Eleazer cried.

"Well, if it is, they know right where your big mouth is, now, don't they?" Silas said.

Josiah put his own whistle to his lips and blew. Silas's head snapped toward him.

"We're surrounded!" Richard said.

Silas gave a laugh, but Josiah could tell it was a nervous one. "They've seen no Indians near Salem Village for months," Silas said.

"Then 'tis other enemies," Richard said. His eyes seemed to grow closer together as he scanned the rocks where William and Ezekiel were hiding.

Josiah held his breath.

"Ha!" Eleazer said as he dropped his shovel. "Then I say we go after them."

Without so much as rustling the grass, Ezekiel and William crept farther from the ditch and blew their whistles again.

"That way!" Richard shouted.

They were off, scrambling toward the sound of the whistles, as Ezekiel and William crept silently in the other direction. In a few seconds, Josiah knew, they would toot again and draw the Putnam cousins that way while they slinked off in another direction. They had promised they could keep that up for a good half hour—and make the Putnams look like fools, too.

So far it was working, but Josiah looked nervously over his shoulder before he blew his whistle again. He hoped his sister was still hiding in the woodshed at Joseph Putnam's place or he was going to look pretty foolish.

Silas hadn't followed his cousins but was standing uncertainly, shovel still in hand, scanning the rocks that edged his father's land. Josiah breathed a prayer before he lifted his head above the rock he was hiding behind. *If it's your will, Lord,* he said silently, *let it be done.*

Silas's mouth fell open when he saw him, but Josiah put his finger to his lips and motioned him over. Silas shook his head.

"I've come from my sister, Hope," Josiah said quietly. "She wants to meet with you."

Silas took a few steps toward him and then stopped. He pulled his lips into a knot before he spoke. "How do I know this is not a trap?" he said.

Josiah was glad the Merry Band of boys had thought of that. He pulled a piece of bark from his pouch and tossed it to him.

Silas picked it up, and his face clouded when he saw the words printed on it. He studied it furiously, his lips moving, and Josiah held back a groan. The note he had written for Hope, with her signature on it, wouldn't do much good if Silas couldn't read.

But Silas seemed to latch on to something he knew, because his face lit up. "H—for Hope!" he said. His face glowed as pink as the sunrise, and Josiah had to force himself not to shake his head in confusion. Silas looked as if he had just seen a whole apple pie all for himself, rather than Hope's name. Josiah knew he would never understand that.

There was no time to ponder it now. He could still hear Ezekiel and William whistling away, while Richard and Eleazer shouted orders to each other. If he waited too long, there would be little time left for Hope and Silas to talk.

"If you want to see her," Josiah whispered, "follow me."

Silas nodded eagerly, and Josiah led him quickly to the

woodshed that stood almost as elegantly as the house on the edge of Joseph Putnam's property.

Josiah had assured Hope that Joseph Putnam always brought in his wood for the breakfast fire the night before. She and Silas would be safe there for quite some time.

Carefully, he opened the door a crack, and Hope sprang from the corner with her face lit up even brighter than Silas's. It faded when she saw her brother.

"Did . . . did you . . . ?" she stammered.

"He's here," Josiah returned.

"Where?"

"Here!" Silas said, poking his head in through the doorway.

She smiled. He smiled. And Josiah shook his head and backed out of the woodshed. As he sat down outside and heard the murmur of their voices inside, he wondered what could be so exciting to Silas about a girl. Especially Hope! She was bossy, crafty, and restless. Josiah thought, *If I wanted to spend time with a girl—which, of course, I don't—it would be someone nice, like Betty Parris*.

Suddenly, there was a whistle, this time close by. It was William's signal that time had run out. Josiah scrambled up and rapped his knuckles against the side of the woodshed. Seconds later, Silas bolted out and looked at Josiah for instructions.

"They'll be back to your farm any minute," Josiah whispered to him.

Silas nodded. "I shall tell them I found a nest of whippoorwills and that's where the whistling was coming from. They're stupid enough to believe that."

As he ran off toward his farm, Josiah watched him in amazement. Maybe he *was* different from the other Putnams.

"Josiah?" a soft voice said behind him. He turned to see Hope, face shining like a newly polished pewter plate. "Thank you," she said.

"Ach. 'Twas nothing."

"It wasn't! And Josiah—" She curled her fingers gently around his arm. "I was right. He is a good person."

Josiah let out a relieved puff of air. Good, then. It was over. She had gathered her information. She could tell Papa what she knew. Josiah could go back to learning to start a fire with flint and a knife and—

"I'd like to talk to him some more," Hope said. Josiah stared at her as she smiled. "Will you help me?" she said.

Chapter Nine

hen the drummer called the Salem Village people to Sunday Meeting the next morning, Josiah still hadn't answered Hope's question.

"She wants us to do it again!" he hissed to Ezekiel and William as he slipped into his seat in the upstairs church gallery. He looked around cautiously for Deacon Edward Putnam, whose job it was to keep all the boys quiet in the loft while the service went on below. If the deacon caught so much as a whisper, he would bring his long tithing pole soundly down on the head of the troublemaker.

Ezekiel nodded as if he were ready to go to work that instant, but William and Josiah looked at each other doubtfully. Josiah glanced at Deacon Putnam, who was busy scolding Richard Putnam's tiny brother Andrew for sniffing too loudly.

"I don't know," Josiah whispered. "They'd be ready for us a second time."

The congregation stood up, and they knew Reverend Parris was entering. As the boys stood with them, William said to Josiah in a muffled voice, "'Tis too dangerous." His eyes darted toward the end of their row.

Josiah's eyes followed them. He saw Eleazer and Richard and . . . Josiah stifled a gasp. There, just a few boys down, was Jonathon Putnam, Nathaniel Putnam's oldest son. It was the first time Josiah had seen him since the three cousins had been released from the Salem Town jail.

Jonathon was the leader of the Putnam boys, and it was easy to see why. He was the tallest, the smartest, and definitely the meanest. Josiah had seen him take down all three of his cousins with one slap of his hand.

Jonathon seemed to feel Josiah's eyes on him, for he looked up at him, and his wide Putnam face narrowed into a scowl until it looked like the blade of an ax. If possible, Jonathon Putnam had grown even meaner in jail.

Hope has done enough, Josiah decided as he quickly looked away. Below, there was a long prayer and then a Psalm, and then the people settled onto their hard seats as bald Deacon Ingersoll turned over the hourglass and Reverend Parris began his sermon.

Josiah sighed and fixed his eyes on the minister. He always tried to pay attention to what was said. But after a few sentences from the reverend, whined out like those of a spoiled child who wasn't getting his way, Josiah's mind always wandered. It took less than one sentence for that to happen today.

As he scanned the people lined up in their seats below, Josiah's eye caught on Betty, and to her right, her cousin

Abigail. Betty was watching her father as if he were about to perform some kind of miracle, but Abigail—

Josiah's eyes widened. No, it couldn't be!

As Abigail's hand sprang to her mouth and her shoulders shook, Josiah knew it was true. Abigail Williams was laughing in church!

And Reverend Parris thinks I'm *a child of the devil*, Josiah grumbled to himself.

His eyes wandered to the other side of the Meeting House where the men sat. It wasn't hard to find his father among them, his broad shoulders rising above those of Benjamin and Giles Porter and Joseph Putnam—and certainly above those of the other Putnams, Josiah noted with pride.

Then he shook his head slightly. If they were going to have peace with those people, he was going to have to stop thinking of them as the enemy. Though after all they had done, that was going to be hard.

Even now, as Josiah watched, Thomas Putnam nudged the elbow of his brother Nathaniel and nodded his head toward Joseph Hutchinson. Nathaniel looked at Papa, too, and both of them lifted their lips like horses who smelled something bad in a trough. Josiah could feel the hair on the back of his neck prickling up, and he hoped his father didn't see the Putnams' sneers.

Papa, it seemed, was listening to every word that squeezed painfully out of Reverend Parris's throat. But the Putnams' eyes were so hard on him that Josiah decided he must have felt the weight of them. Josiah held his breath as his father turned, looked, and smiled.

The Putnams, it appeared, were as surprised as he was.

Nathaniel cleared his throat, and Thomas started forward as if Papa had jumped up and waved a musket at him.

It occurred to Josiah then that he had been so busy with Hope's work that he hadn't thought to listen for clues to what had happened at the meeting in the Hutchinsons' kitchen the night before last. Obviously, no peace had been found.

Josiah felt a poke at his ribs, and he looked at William, who was nodding toward Reverend Parris.

"Two nights past," the minister was saying, "many of us gathered in the home of a dweller in this village. The meeting was called in the disguise of a call to peace—"

Disguise! Josiah nearly lurched from his seat. William grabbed one arm and Ezekiel took hold of the other.

"But it was nothing more than an attack on the leader of this flock," Samuel Parris went on. He put his hand to his chest so no one could miss the fact that he was talking about himself. "My very motives—my intentions toward this congregation—were questioned! How can this be? Am I not due respect by the very virtue of my office, without having to explain why I do as I do?"

Reverend Parris waved his fist, and the entire congregation seemed to hold its breath. He was shaking his fist right at Joseph Hutchinson.

"I should be honored, not shamed, for the work I try to do here! I will no longer stand the attacks of jealous men who would tear me from this pulpit and drive me from town while pretending to want to make peace with me and those who support my ministry."

In the gathering below, all eyes turned to Joseph Hutchinson. Up in the gallery, for the first time in his life,

Josiah wanted to hurt someone. He wanted to stand and throw his fists into Jonathon Putnam's face, his knee into Richard Putnam's stomach, and his shoulder into Eleazer Putnam's chest. If the minister could hurt his father this way, what was the difference if he hurled every one of their enemies' sons over the railing?

But he kept his eyes, now filling with angry tears, on his father. Whatever Papa did, that's what he would do as well.

Reverend Parris whined on, shamelessly quoting Papa's beloved Bible to make him sound like Judas himself. And through it all, Joseph Hutchinson sat straight up. Before Josiah's eyes, his shoulders seemed to get bigger and his head to stretch taller. While everyone else shriveled under the minister's harsh words, it was as if his father grew—until it looked as if he could carry the weight of all these mistaken people on his broad back.

Josiah tried to sit taller on his seat. From the end of the row, he heard a soft snort, and he looked to see Jonathon Putnam's eyes riveted on him. A smirk played at the corners of his mouth, and he nodded toward the minister.

You know he's right, his bulging Putnam eyes seemed to say.

No, he's wrong, Josiah's eyes said back. And he didn't take them off of Jonathon until the smirking boy looked away.

There were two services every Sunday, with a break for dinner in between. Josiah dashed down to the churchyard as soon as the last prayer of the first service was over to follow his family home. He was certain they wouldn't be returning for the second. He wondered if they would ever be returning.

There was a heavy rumbling of whispers as Josiah made his way around the long skirts and leather boots toward the edge of the churchyard that bordered the Meeting House property. He just wanted to get home and away from their suspicious eyes.

Moving swiftly, he heard a "Psst!" that seemed directed at him.

The sound would have been lost among the gossiping if a hand hadn't snatched at his sleeve. He looked up to see Silas beside him. He wasn't looking at Josiah, but he talked out of the corner of his mouth toward Josiah.

"I don't agree with Reverend Parris," he said. "Your father, he's a good man."

Josiah wasn't sure the shock in his head would have allowed him to answer anyway, even if someone hadn't snickered from a few feet away.

"Silas! What are you about?" the irritated voice said.

Both Silas and Josiah jerked their heads toward Jonathon Putnam. He stood with his hands planted on his narrow hips, his eyes dripping with hate.

"Get away from him," he said to Silas. "He's a disease— just like his father!"

Silas slunk away, but Josiah didn't move. He only glared at Jonathon Putnam. For the second time that morning, the powerful urge to hurt someone swept over him. He wanted to smash into Jonathon, and he wanted to do it now.

With the parsonage only a few yards away, Josiah lunged forward. But his arm was caught by a set of iron fingers.

"Whoa there," a low voice breathed in his ear. "Don't bring more shame on your father than he's already suffered today."

Josiah whipped around to face Giles Porter. Where on earth had he come from? He tried to pull his arm away, but Giles held fast. "Don't worry, boy," Giles said. His eyes shifted toward Jonathon Putnam, who was retreating into the church. "I'll see that your father has justice. You leave it to me."

Giles's words didn't sound comforting. They sounded like an order that Jonathon Putnam would issue.

Josiah rubbed his arm where Giles had held it and watched him melt back into the muttering villagers, none of whom realized that a battle had threatened to break loose in the midst of them. As he watched Giles flash his charming smile at Mama and put his hand on Papa's shoulder, Josiah shuddered.

It didn't look like peace at all. It looked like war.

Chapter Ten

The air that Sunday evening was as heavy as Joseph Hutchinson's mood. Hope and Josiah retreated to the front step right after supper—to find a cool breeze and get away from the deep sighs that heaved from their father's chest as he sat in his chair and gripped its arms with his hands.

As Josiah sat down next to Hope, he was sure Papa was thinking about Reverend Parris as he squeezed his chair. Josiah slapped miserably at a mosquito that had already planted itself on his skin.

"I spoke to Betty Parris after the first service today," Hope said.

Josiah stopped. "About what?" he said slowly.

"I asked her to get a message to Silas that I would meet him at Joseph Putnam's woodshed again tomorrow."

"Hope—"

"Didn't you hear what Reverend Parris said this morning, right in front of everyone? It's more important than ever now that we get people on our side, especially people who used to be our enemies."

Josiah narrowed his eyes at her. "That's not why you want to talk to Silas," he said.

Hope tilted her chin at him. "It wasn't before. But now it's part of the reason—and the most important part. We have to help Papa or *he'll* be the one run out of town, not Samuel Parris."

Josiah looked hard at his sister. Hope Hutchinson might be stubborn, always insisting on doing things her own way, but he had never known her to outright lie. She was a good person. She would never use Papa's fight to get what she wanted.

"What are you thinking, Josiah Hutchinson?" she said. Her black eyes began to snap. "Do you doubt my word?"

"No!" Josiah said quickly. Perhaps she wanted to talk to Silas again because she liked him, but that wasn't the only reason.

"Good evening there!" a voice interrupted.

Josiah and Hope looked up to see two men coming across the yard toward them. A chill went up Josiah's spine. It was Ezekiel Cheever, the village constable, and John Willard, his deputy. The Hutchinson children stood up nervously. The only time these men came around was when there was trouble with the law.

Cheever, as usual, didn't say a word but scanned the area with his eyes, as if thieves and murderers lurked behind every bush. Papa always said the short, round-bellied man took his job a little too seriously.

But John Willard smiled at them until tiny wrinkles appeared at the corners of his eyes. He even tipped his hat slightly to Hope.

"Is your papa at home?" he said.

"Aye, he's within," Hope said.

"Will you tell him we're here to see him?"

Hope nodded, but she didn't move.

"You've naught to worry, Miss Hutchinson," Willard said. "He's not in trouble. We've only come to question him as we're questioning all the villagers."

Josiah had never heard anyone call Hope "Miss Hutchinson" before. He was sure that was why Hope smiled back as she stepped aside to let the deputy pass.

Papa, however, did not smile when he saw the constables enter the kitchen. Josiah watched from the hearth as his father stood up, both fists unfolding and then doubling up again.

"Good evening," Papa said stiffly. "What might I do for you?"

"We've come to ask you some questions, if we may," Cheever said. It was the first time he had spoken, and Josiah remembered at once how sharp his voice was. He spoke as if his tongue had spikes.

"We're asking these same questions of all the villagers," John Willard hurried to put in. "At the request of Reverend Parris."

Papa's eyes turned to stone, and for a moment Josiah thought he was going to toss both constables out of the house.

But Papa sat again and motioned for Willard and Cheever to choose chairs. Mama hurried to bring cider, but Cheever waved her off. This was official business, not a friendly visit.

"I will answer your questions," Papa said, "but first I must know what this is about."

"Now Hutchinson—" Cheever began.

But Willard put up his hand and leaned his long body toward Papa. The crinkles at his eyes were still there. "It seems that sometime today, someone broke into Reverend Parris's study at the parsonage and took some papers."

"Papers?" Papa said.

"Aye, some sealed documents. He wouldn't say what they were, only that they were important."

Josiah sharply sucked in air. Sealed documents. Could those be the papers he had seen that day on Reverend Parris's desk? Those bundles of parchment with their blue wax P's?

"What would anyone want with such things?" Papa said.

Cheever and Willard exchanged glances, and for no reason he could name, Josiah felt his stomach churn.

"The reverend says someone might try to use them to take his ministry from him," Willard said finally.

Papa gave a hard laugh. "What are they, testaments that he committed murder?"

"What do you mean?" Cheever said sharply. He scraped his chair back and stood over Papa.

"I mean nothing," Papa said. "Sit down, Cheever, and don't get puffed up. Reverend Parris has thought there was a plot to overtake him since the moment he set foot in Salem Village. You heard him ranting about it from the pulpit this morning." Papa shook his head sadly. "I have tried to see some good in the man, but now I fear he's going mad right before our eyes."

"Then you do want him out?" Cheever said.

Papa shot him a stern look, and Willard put his hand on Cheever's arm. Josiah felt Hope's hand creep over onto his own sleeve. Mama moved quietly to stand beside them.

"Get on with your questions and be gone," their father said.

"All right, then," Willard said. "You did not attend the second service today, eh?"

"Nay."

"Where did you go immediately following the first meeting?"

"Here."

"As you sat here—across from the parsonage—did you see anyone other than Reverend Parris or his family or servants go to or from their house?"

"Nay."

"Did you yourself go near the parsonage?"

Papa sat up straight in his chair. His knuckles were white from gripping the arms.

"No," he said woodenly.

Willard's eyes swept over Josiah and Hope, then returned to Papa. "To your knowledge, did any member of your family go near the parsonage?"

Joseph Hutchinson banged his feet onto the floor and stood to tower over the constables. Both of them shrank back in their chairs, and Hope clutched at Josiah's sleeve with a sweaty hand.

"You say you are questioning all the villagers?" Papa said in a low warning voice that Josiah knew all too well.

"Aye, Joseph," Willard said.

"Are you asking all of them these same insulting questions?"

"Joseph, I only do what Reverend Parris instructs—"

"Did he instruct you to accuse me of stealing from him?"

With each question, Papa's voice grew quieter. It was like a calm before thunder and lightning were unleashed. Josiah stiffened his shoulders and waited.

"He is somewhat suspicious—"

Papa slammed his hand flat on the table and stopped not only Willard's words but every other sound in the kitchen. No one even breathed.

"I know you to be a good man, John," Papa said to him. "And you, too, Cheever, for all your high and mighty posturing. So I advise you to stop taking your instructions from Reverend Parris and start taking them from God. Because it seems that only He can save this village from destruction now."

"Hutchinson," Ezekiel Cheever said.

But again John Willard put his hand on the constable's arm and this time pulled him out of the chair and steered him toward the door. "Let us leave the man," he said. "Good evening, Joseph. Goody Hutchinson."

The deputy nodded to them all and hurried from the room with Cheever at his heels. Neither of them looked back, and Josiah could only wonder where they would go from here. To Reverend Parris to report on his father? Perhaps to Thomas Putnam? Or did they take Papa's advice and go to God?

"Get you to bed, children," Papa said when the front door had closed. "'Tis late."

Although it was, in fact, barely dusk, neither Hope nor Josiah uttered a word of protest as they headed for the stairs. Papa had things to say to their mother, things they weren't meant to hear.

Up in their room, Josiah plopped himself down on the blanket chest under the window and looked out, but Cheever and Willard had already disappeared. Hope began to pace furiously.

"Papa is right!" she whispered loudly to Josiah. "Reverend Parris *has* gone mad! Accusing Papa of stealing his precious papers! It was the Putnams, of course!"

"Why would the Putnams want papers to drive Parris out of town?" Josiah said. "Papa always says they need him to get power in the church."

"I don't care," Hope said stubbornly. "If there's trouble, the Putnams are at the bottom of it."

Suddenly, she stopped pacing, and a light began to dawn on her face. Josiah watched her carefully.

"Josiah!" she said. She scooted to the chest and nudged him over. He could feel her body shaking with excitement as she sank down beside him. "Silas is on our side. I know he is."

"Aye," Josiah said. It certainly seemed so.

"If the Putnams are behind this, it's sure he knows about it—and it's certain I can convince him to tell me." Her eyes were shining like two flames.

"You think so?" Josiah said.

"Aye. I'll ask him tomorrow morning." She looked Josiah full in the face. "He's to meet me in the woodshed. Will you come and stand watch? Please?"

The thoughts hammered inside Josiah's head. It seemed the perfect solution. But what if it really was a trap? What if Silas was just pretending to like Hope and hate his cousins? *Then it's a pretty complicated plot!* the other thoughts told him. He remembered now—Silas hadn't been sitting next to the other Putnams in the gallery that morning. And the anger in Jonathon's eyes when he saw Silas talking to Josiah had been real.

"All right," Josiah said finally. "But only this once, Hope. This isn't a game anymore."

The flames went out in Hope's eyes, and she nodded sadly. "I know it. After Silas helps us, I have to tell Papa. People are going to jail over these things, Josiah."

"Aye."

The room grew quiet. Only the urgent rise and fall of their parents' voices came, muffled, through the floor.

Josiah began to pray silently. *I think this is your will, God,* he said. *You seem to have led us to it.* He could hear soft murmurs coming from Hope's lips. He wondered if she was praying, too.

Before they went to their beds, Josiah agreed that he and Hope would get up before dawn and go to the woodshed at Joseph Putnam's. He was so afraid he wouldn't wake up in time that he woke up every few minutes during the night and peered out the window to see if it was growing light yet. He finally fell into a deep sleep in the wee hours of the morning and was awakened not by Hope's voice in his ear, but his father's.

"Josiah," Papa said as he shook his shoulder.

Josiah jolted up in bed and tried to sort out his father's face from his dreams. It was still so dark in the room that he could barely see it.

"You must get up now and be about your work so you can go to the sawmill and help Giles and Benjamin today."

Josiah nodded, but his thoughts were still in a jumble. Work in the sawmill? All day?

"I must go to Salem Town and talk to Phillip English," Papa said.

At the shipowner's name, Josiah came fully awake. Phillip English was Papa's wealthy friend, with whom he traded lumber and other goods. Josiah had lived with him last summer, and he knew how much Papa respected Phillip's business sense. The Putnams had often accused Papa of being greedy because he had made so much money dealing with Mr. English. Something important must be taking Papa to him.

"I shall be gone all day," Papa said. "Tell Benjamin that, and see you do just as Giles tells you. I don't want this trip to hamper our work at the mill."

"Aye, sir," Josiah said, though he wanted to throw off his covers and shout, "No! I'll never work for Giles Porter! I don't trust him!"

But even if he'd had the courage, he wouldn't have been so stupid. He noticed now, as his eyes grew used to the darkness, that Papa looked as if he hadn't slept. There were bags of dark skin under his eyes that reminded Josiah of his whistle pouch. Josiah would work for Giles Porter, then, for Papa's sake.

But as the door closed behind his father and Hope whipped open her bed curtains, another horror struck him.

Hope scrambled over to his cot. "What about Silas?" she whispered.

"Can you not meet him tomorrow?" Josiah said. "Maybe that would give him more time to learn information about Reverend Parris's papers anyway."

"But how would I let him know I'm not coming? He would think I didn't want to see him—or that we were setting a trap for him!"

Josiah tried to think of an answer, but there were too many questions crowding his head. Hope stood and straightened her shoulders the way Papa did.

"I'll go alone, then," she said.

"Hope, you can't!"

"I've naught to be afraid of, Josiah." She hurried to her wardrobe and flung open its doors. "Silas would never hurt me. I know that."

"It isn't Silas I'm worried about," Josiah whispered back.

"Josiah!" said a deep voice from outside the door. "Get you gone."

Josiah felt his stomach turn into a knot as he looked at his sister. "See you be careful," he said.

She glanced back at him and gave him a strange look. "Aye," she said. "God will be with me."

It wasn't until he had finished his chores and was on his way to the sawmill that Josiah realized what that look was. It was the look of a grown-up.

✠ ⋅✠⋅ ✠

Chapter Eleven

osiah had barely left the farm when he heard hoofbeats behind him. It was odd for anyone to be out on a horse so early in the morning, and Josiah's heart quickened as he stepped off the road to let it pass. But the horse slowed down—and so did Josiah's heartbeat when he saw that the two riders were girls. A moment later, his stomach tightened as he realized who the girls were. Ann Putnam Jr., Richard's sister, reined the horse to a stop, though it was Abigail Williams behind her who did the talking.

"Going in the wrong direction, aren't you, boy?" she said, without a trace of sleep in her voice.

Do these people never rest? Josiah thought. *They must stay up all night thinking of things to do to make trouble for us.*

"We thought you would be off looking for Silas," Abigail added.

Josiah looked up abruptly, and when he saw Abigail look

triumphantly at the spidery Ann, he knew his face was giving him away. He tried to hide his surprise as he said, "I don't know what you're talking about. I'm going to the sawmill."

"Of course," Abigail said, her green eyes aimed at him like the barrel of a gun. "You Hutchinsons are a greedy lot."

"Aye," Ann said.

If she ever had a thought of her own, Josiah didn't know what it would be.

"But where is your sister going this morning?" Abigail said.

Josiah willed himself to not look around to see if Hope was at that moment sneaking past them toward Joseph Putnam's woodshed.

"To her work, I suppose," Josiah said evenly. "What business is it of yours?"

"Plenty," Abigail said. "You'd best get back to your house—if she is indeed there—and give her a message."

Josiah sighed impatiently. "What message?"

"From Jonathon," Ann said. She smiled at Abigail as if she had just contributed something important to the conversation.

"Tell her to stay away from Silas Putnam," Abigail said. Her voice was as narrow and mean as her eyes. It was all he could do not to dash back to the farmhouse and beg Hope to stay put. But something about the way the two girls smirked at each other held him back, and he stepped toward the horse.

"Your cousin Jonathon has sent you on a useless turkey hunt," Josiah said to Ann. "What would Hope want with a Putnam? You've never meant anything but trouble for us."

Ann's face immediately went blank. "But Jonathon told us—"

"Shut it, Ann," Abigail snapped. She kept her eyes on Josiah. "If Jonathon says he saw Silas smile at her between services yesterday, then he saw it." She leaned toward him, almost crushing Ann against the horse's neck. "And if he says he saw Silas talking to you, then he saw it. What else is he to think but that there is something going on among you three, especially after Silas betrayed them all last spring when your sister brought that false accusation against them?"

"Besides," Ann said, "we just saw someone running through the shadows toward Wolf Pits Meadow. Could that have been your sister going to meet Silas?"

Abigail stabbed her sharply in the back with her fingernail. "It *was* his sister, of course."

"Well, we couldn't quite see her clearly, but . . . "

"It *was* your sister," Abigail said to Josiah, though he was sure the anger in her voice was as much for Ann as it was for him.

But that was all right. Ann had said enough for him to know that they weren't sure it was Hope they had seen, and they didn't know where she was going. She would be safely in the woodshed, or even back home, before they could get their uncertain news back to Jonathon, especially if Josiah kept them here for a few minutes.

He glanced anxiously at the sky. The sun was making its way through the trees, and Giles and Benjamin would be waiting for Papa. Maybe just one minute. That would probably be long enough.

"So, what say you, boy?" Abigail said.

Josiah rewarded them both with a grin. "I say you tie up your horse there on that oak, and you go into our henhouse.

You'll find Hope there, gathering eggs for our mother. I'm surprised you're not home doing the same thing, Ann. Of course, you, Abigail, never have to stoop to such things."

"No," Abigail said, arching her neck like a queen.

"I wonder if that would change, though," Josiah went on, still grinning, "if it somehow got back to your uncle that you were seen *laughing* during church yesterday."

Ann looked at Abigail as if she had just grown a second nose. "Abby!" she said.

"Don't be a ninny, Ann. I did nothing of the kind." She bared her teeth at Josiah. "And even if I did, who would believe *him?*"

"I'd never tell, of course," Josiah said. "But Betty might."

"Betty!" Abigail cried.

"Aye. She saw it, too. She was sitting right next to you."

Abigail made a raspy sound that Josiah was fairly certain was her version of a laugh. "That little rabbit knows better than to say a word against me."

"But who do you think your uncle would believe?" Josiah said. "You or his daughter?" Josiah knew he was enjoying himself too much, but just one more stab at Abigail, and then he would be gone. "After all," he said, "everyone knows that Reverend Parris loves his own daughter more than anyone. Especially you."

For an instant, he thought she was going to spring from the horse and put her hands around his throat. She might well have, he knew, if Ann hadn't flung her arm against her and cut in with her shaky voice.

"Your threats don't scare us, Josiah Hutchinson," Ann said. She wheeled the horse around and dug her heels into its sides. "They don't scare us at all."

But from the speed at which they galloped toward the Hutchinson farm, Josiah was pretty sure they did . . . at least a little.

He lingered for only a second longer. Should he go after Hope and warn her and Silas?

No, he decided. If he went for the woodshed, he would give their location away. Surely, he had given them enough time. Hope knew she had to be back before long or Mama would be wondering where she was. He smiled to himself, remembering that the Putnam boys would be at Edward's digging their precious ditches.

When Josiah gave his father's message to Benjamin Porter, he and Giles traded worried looks. But Giles flashed a smile at once and took Josiah by the shoulder.

"Come along, then, boy," he said cheerfully. "I taught you how to plow. It's sure I can teach you how to hold a log for cutting."

You never taught me anything! Josiah wanted to say. But he bit his lip and followed Giles to the cutting room.

The morning seemed to drag on. Between listening to Giles bark constant orders at him and wondering if Hope had returned home without running into the two spider women on horseback, it seemed that dinnertime would never come.

It was nearly noon when he went to the window for the tenth time to check where the sun was.

"Have you some more important business to attend to, boy?" Giles said to him. Irritation chewed at the edges of his voice.

"Nay," Josiah said, and he hurried back to the giant saw.

Giles had just secured a half log on the rack, and he pulled the lever that started the blade. Josiah was glad. He wouldn't be able to hear Giles over the whirring.

Giles pointed with his free hand, and Josiah grabbed on to the log to catch the piece that would fall from the rack once the blade cut it in half.

Almost noon, he thought. *I can run home and find out from Hope what happened to Silas. It's certain I'm worryin' for nothing. . . .*

Suddenly, a shout from Giles broke over the racket of the saw blade. Josiah looked up . . . and felt a tear at his arms.

The big piece of wood had tumbled from the rack, and its newly cut edge hit the undersides of Josiah's forearms as he held them out. Blood trickled from his left arm like the opening to an underground spring.

The blade whirred to a stop, and Josiah thought he heard Giles swear under his breath as he jumped the log rack and hurried toward him.

"Why did you not pay attention?" he shouted. Too roughly, he pulled Josiah's bleeding arm to inspect the damage.

"What is it?" Benjamin cried as he ran into the cutting room. "Ach! Are you all right, son?" he said to Josiah.

"Aye," Josiah said tightly. *And thank you for asking, Giles,* he added in his mind.

Both bent over Josiah's arms. The skin on the right one was only scraped and raw, but the left one was still bleeding. Benjamin whipped a handkerchief from inside his shirt and wrapped it around the cut.

"Take him to Prudence," he said to Giles. "She's fixed up wounded boys before."

He smiled at Josiah, but Josiah could feel Giles scowling at him.

"Clumsy boy," Giles muttered. But the charm was back on his face as he led Josiah toward the Porters' house. "It seems you can't take on any job without trying to cut off a limb, can you, boy?" he said.

Josiah's thoughts reeled back to the incident last spring, when he had been pulling stumps from the field and ended up almost crippling himself.

"I shall be all right," Josiah said. He didn't try to hide the anger in his voice. "I can find Goody Porter myself. You can go back to work."

Giles wiggled his eyebrows. "Ah, 'tis a saucy boy, is it?" He stopped and surveyed Josiah's face. "Good, then," he said. "Go on to Prudence, and see you stay there until I come to check on you."

He turned and hurried back to the mill, and Josiah couldn't resist making a sour face at his back. *You think you're the master of me, don't you, Giles Porter?* Josiah thought.

Prudence Porter clucked like a chicken over Josiah's arm as she guided him to a table in the corner of the kitchen and nudged him to sit in a chair.

"This is Giles's desk," she told Josiah. "He sits here to go over his business, and from time to time he'll smoke a pipe. . . . "

Her voice trailed off as she pawed through the items on Giles's "desk" until she found a cloth bag. She opened it and pulled out two brownish leaves.

"Have you ever seen tobacco?" she said.

Josiah shook his head and watched curiously as Prudence

spit on the two brown leaves and stuck them on the worst of his wounds.

Her voice lowered to a hoarse whisper. "Spring a year ago, when I was helping your mother and that Quaker woman take care of your sister, the woman told me tobacco wet with spittle could keep a wound from festering." She patted the poultice proudly. "You're the first one I've tried it on. Let's see if she was right."

Josiah wasn't sure why she felt she had to whisper when she was talking about the widow. If Faith Hooker had said this strange cure would work, it was good enough for him.

"Now, you sit right here, and I shall gather a bit of bugloss for some soup," she said.

Josiah tried not to groan as she took her basket and hurried out to her herb garden. Not only did he hate bugloss soup, but it took forever to make. She was obviously planning to keep him there all day. He had to get home and talk to Hope.

He sighed. He wouldn't argue with his own mother, and he wasn't allowed to argue with *any* grown-up. He wished Ezekiel would come in and keep him company.

Josiah stirred uneasily in the chair and looked over the table where he was sitting.

Giles Porter's desk. For doing business. For the sawmill? Josiah wondered. He had always thought his father handled all of that. Josiah frowned. He didn't like the idea of Giles touching anything that touched the Hutchinson family.

Josiah tried not to look at Giles's papers, but his eyes seemed to be drawn to them. There were stacks of things neatly lined up in rows—and all parchment. He remembered

Reverend Parris's desk and shook his head. Where did people get all this paper? His father rarely used a piece unless it was terribly important.

Josiah was about to look away in disgust when his eye caught on something that wasn't parchment. It was blue. And waxy. And shaped like a P.

He gasped. Reverend Parris's papers, hidden here beneath the sawmill business on Giles Porter's desk!

Josiah's thoughts went wild. *Should I take them to Papa? Should I leave them here and send Papa to find them? Should I—*

"Well, well," a voice broke in, "you've taken some of my private stock, have you?"

Josiah's thoughts stopped spinning, and he looked up at Giles Porter with his heart in his mouth.

"I've taken nothing!" he cried.

"Indeed you have." Giles gave an automatic smile and pointed to the tobacco poultice on Josiah's arm. "I'll be one pipeful short come winter, eh?"

Josiah had to press his knees together to keep them from shaking. He didn't answer. He knew his voice would tremble too hard for him to speak.

"Prudence says she wants you to eat soup," Giles said, "but I say you can do that as easily at home, eh?"

"Aye." Josiah managed to get out. That would be perfect. He could get home and tell Papa what he had seen. It didn't matter now that the Porters were their friends. He knew his father had long pushed aside his doubts about Giles's honesty, but he needed all the information now, if he were going to do God's will.

"I shall be off, then," Josiah said. "Please thank Goody Porter for her help."

"I will." Giles looked amused as he opened the door for Josiah. "Some boys will do anything to get away from work, eh?"

"Aye," Josiah forced himself to say. "I suppose."

He tried to walk slowly until he was sure Giles was no longer watching him. Then he broke into a run toward the Hutchinson farm. He had to get to Papa—fast.

He almost slammed into the ground as he rounded the curve that brought the farm into sight. As he looked toward the barn, he could see the wagon wasn't there. Then he remembered—Papa had said he would be gone all day. How was he going to keep what he had found locked up inside him until Papa returned? How was he going to keep Hope and Mama from knowing that he had an awful secret?

It looked as if he was going to be put to the test right away, for his mother opened the front door as he walked across the yard.

"Josiah!" she called to him.

At the sound of the worry in her voice, Josiah picked up his feet and ran to her.

"Josiah," she said. Her eyes were streaming. "Do you know where your sister is?"

An awful tingling began at the base of his spine and slowly moved upward. "No," he said. "Why?"

"Because she's not here," Mama replied. "She's not been here all day."

✢ ✢ ✢

Chapter Twelve

eborah Hutchinson's face was waxy and pale as her eyes begged Josiah for information about Hope. The fear went up Josiah's spine like fire up a rope, and he knew there could be no sneaking. Not now. Not ever again.

"She went to Joseph Putnam's woodshed," he said. "She went to meet Silas Putnam."

There was no anger in Mama's wet, red eyes as she took Josiah's shoulders.

"Is she safe with him, Josiah? He took her side once. Can he be trusted?"

"Aye, Mama," Josiah said.

"Go there, then, and fetch her home," she said. Her voice shook, but somehow it was firm, too. "Can you do that without the Putnams ... without those other boys ...?"

"Aye," Josiah said, and before she could see the doubt he

felt, he turned and ran, his toes digging into the ground, toward Joseph Putnam's.

Perhaps Hope fell asleep in the woodshed, he told himself as he hurried on. *We neither of us got much sleep last night.*

But as soon as the thoughts flipped through his head, he tossed them aside. He should have gone to her this morning, as soon as Abigail and Ann had warned him. He should have gotten to her and told her to stay away.

As his footsteps turned toward Wolf Pits Meadow, he heard the bushes to his left rustle. *I can't stop for deer,* he thought frantically. *I can't stop for anything!*

But the "deer" that leaped in front of him had only two legs—and they belonged to Ann Putnam Jr.

"Leave me be, Ann," he said fiercely. He tried to push past her, but she clung to his sleeve. The urge to hurt someone he had felt so often lately seized him again. He wanted to shove Ann into the dirt as he moved on, but she was a girl. If it had been her brother who stood there taunting him . . .

"We warned you, Josiah Hutchinson," she said. "We told you to keep your sister away from Silas."

Josiah yanked his arm back, and the pain from his cut surged through him. He held his arm against his chest so she couldn't see the poultice through his sleeve.

She looked at him as if he were a piece of spice cake she couldn't wait to bite into. "You cannot say we didn't warn you."

Josiah's mind was whirling, but he tried to catch hold. "So tell me more," he said. "What was to become of her if she saw Silas?"

Ann all but licked her chops. This, Josiah saw, was the most delicious piece of information she had ever passed along. Josiah twisted his mouth in disgust.

"It was to be the end of Hope Hutchinson," she said. "That's what Jonathon told us last night."

Josiah's mouth went slack. He stepped forward and grabbed her—girl or not—hard by the shoulders and pulled her to him.

"What do you mean?" he shouted into her startled face. "The end of her how, where?"

Ann wriggled and shook loose from Josiah's weak arm. She backed up, and her thin lips came open in an ugly slit. "They're taking her away someplace!" she said, spitting the words at him. "They're taking her someplace—and leaving her to die!"

With that, she got her other arm free and, clutching her skirts in her arms, took off like a musket shot toward her farm.

Josiah didn't go after her. He could only stand, stunned, at the edge of Wolf Pits Meadow and feel the fear burn its final inch to his brain. She had said they were going to let Hope die somewhere, and nothing had ever seemed more clear to him. They would certainly do it.

Josiah squeezed his eyes shut and held his throbbing arm to him. A plan. He needed a plan, and there was no time to get William or Ezekiel to help him. And what would they do anyway? Who—who could help?

Josiah broke from his frozen stance and looked across the meadows to where he had been headed. Joseph Putnam. Of course.

He clutched his arm tighter and ran as best he could. Another thing was sure. They hadn't told Ann Putnam Jr. to tell him as much as she had. She was always blabbering more than she should, and this time Abigail was not there to stop her. He still had surprise on his side. Joseph Putnam would help him decide how to use that.

Hold on, Hope! he thought as he stumbled on. *Hold on— and pray.*

Josiah was praying hard himself as Joseph's white house came into view. *Please let him be on the porch. Please let him come down to meet me.*

"Boy!" someone hissed to him.

Josiah looked around in alarm, but he didn't stop. He was so close. He was nearly there.

"Boy!" came the voice again, and from the long grass on the farthest edge of the meadow, Tituba rose. Her face was shiny black beneath her white cap.

"I can't talk—" Josiah huffed at her.

"Please, my Betty, she say give you dis!" Tituba thrust out a rolled-up piece of parchment. Her face looked as frightened as he knew his did.

Josiah stopped and took it from her. By the time he unrolled it and started to read, Tituba was gone.

It was Betty's round handwriting and her unusual spelling. Josiah had been grateful to see it many times before, but he wasn't sure he was so thankful this time. The message read: "Silus sez meet him at the uzule plas."

Josiah wanted to crumple the paper and pitch it at someone. *Uzule?* What was uzule? Why couldn't she learn to spell?

Then it hit him. *Usual! She means the usual place!*

Josiah crammed the note into his whistle pouch with his good hand and headed almost gleefully toward the woodshed.

Meet him at the usual place, he thought. Silas had sent the message through Betty. It had to be all right. Betty would never betray him. Silas would have news. Maybe he would even have Hope.

But as Josiah slammed through the doorway of Joseph Putnam's woodshed with his breath coming out in gasps, the figure who turned to him with a face as pale as gooseflesh was Silas Putnam. No one else was there.

Josiah looked around wildly, as if he hoped to find his sister in a crack in the wall.

"She's not here," Silas said. His voice was brittle. "She never came this morning."

Silas's syrup-colored hair bore the marks of his fingers having been frantically dragged through it a thousand times since dawn.

"Where is she?" Josiah said.

"I don't know."

"You do!" Josiah cried. He stalked across the shed toward Silas until he was backed into a corner. Silas's eyes clouded as he shook his head.

"I don't!" he said tearfully.

"Then why are you here?"

"Because I wanted you to know I had nothing to do with it!"

Josiah stuck his right hand in the middle of Silas's chest and pulled him by his shirt. "Nothing to do with what?" He shook Silas hard. "With *what?*"

"Their plan," he said. "I waited here until the sun was all the way up, and I thought . . . I thought she'd just changed her mind."

"She didn't," Josiah said through his teeth. He tightened

his fingers around Silas's shirtfront.

"I know! I know that now. When I got back to the farm, I could hear all three of them laughing in one of the ditches—Jonathon, Richard, and Eleazer. So I hid behind a rock and listened."

"What did they say?" Josiah cried. He knew if he would stay quiet, Silas would tell him, but somehow he couldn't stop the questions that came from his throat, or the anger that raged through his hand as he shook Silas again.

"Richard told them Ann had gone off early to get Abigail, and they were going to cut off Hope before she got to wherever she was going."

"But they couldn't have!" Josiah said. "I held them off until she could get here."

"You didn't hold them long enough," Silas said. He was crying hard now. "At dinnertime, Ann came riding up on her horse and couldn't wait to get them all aside. They kept telling her to be quiet, and I pretended I didn't hear. But she told them . . . she told them Abigail was waiting . . . with Hope."

"Where?" Josiah said.

"I don't know!"

"Stupid!" Josiah cried. And with a yank of his arm, he sent Silas tumbling across the woodshed.

Silas stayed in a heap in the other corner, quietly sobbing. "I tried to get word to you," Silas choked out. "I made an excuse to go to the Parrises', and I told Betty to get a message to you. Then I came here." He swabbed his face with his sleeve, but the tears kept coming. "I've been waiting for hours. But you never came."

All the anger seeped out of Josiah, and he went slowly

over to Silas. Sinking down next to him, he fought to keep back his own tears.

"You really don't know where she is, do you?" Josiah asked.

Silas shook his head miserably.

"Ann says they're going to take her somewhere—" Josiah's voice snagged on the words. "They're going to leave her to die."

Silas looked at him.

"You think they'll do it, don't you?" Josiah said.

"Aye," Silas said.

Josiah put his head down on his arms. Silas had been his last hope, and now it looked as if that was completely gone—

But no.

Josiah scrambled up and reached his hand down to Silas.

"Come on, then!" he said. "We'll go to your uncle Joseph. He can help us!"

Silas looked doubtfully at Josiah's outstretched hand.

"Are you with us or against us, Silas?" Josiah said. The tears were gone now. There was only decision in his voice.

Silas put his hand up and clasped Josiah's.

Suddenly, a voice came from the doorway. "Ah, now isn't this a pretty picture?"

Silas let go and slid against the wall. Josiah stood still and looked up into Jonathon Putnam's sneering face.

"'Tis true then, eh?" Jonathon said. "You two are . . . kindred spirits?" As he talked, he moved slowly toward Josiah.

Josiah's heart threatened to burst from his chest, but he didn't move. Even when Richard and Eleazer appeared in the doorway behind Jonathon, he didn't move.

"Where is my sister?" Josiah said. "What have you done with her?"

Jonathon stopped and folded his arms across his narrow chest. "Well now, cousins, isn't it interesting that he would show such concern for his sister?" he said. "He didn't seem to care much about her when he allowed her to keep company with evil swine—like this!" He turned with a jerk and kicked Silas square in the stomach.

Silas yelped, and suddenly all the anger Josiah had held back for days surged in him. Wanting to hurl his fists into Jonathon at church, wanting to spit at Giles Porter, wanting to shove Ann to the ground—it all came up and out in one gaping roar as he dove into Jonathon like a mad dog.

For a surprised instant, Jonathon did nothing. But by the second punch that Josiah let fly into his belly, he had sprung back fighting.

"Grab him, Richard!" Jonathon shouted. "Grab him and tear off his arm!"

Josiah felt as if his arm had already been torn off, but he kept pounding at Jonathon with the other one. When he brought his knee up into Jonathon's stomach, the oldest Putnam cousin fell back gasping, but Richard pinned Josiah's two throbbing arms behind his back while Eleazer stepped in and clumsily bloodied his nose with his fist.

Jonathon pulled himself to his feet and watched Josiah struggle against Richard. Eleazer drew back his arm again, but Jonathon grabbed it.

"No," he said. "This one is mine." He jerked his head toward Silas, who was doubled up on the floor. "You may have *him*."

It didn't seem to matter to Eleazer. He pounced toward Silas with bubbles of saliva gathering at the corners of his mouth.

"Silas! Watch out!" Josiah cried.

But he never saw whether his warning helped or not. Jonathon threw a punch that sent Josiah into a dark tunnel.

Chapter Thirteen

hen Josiah opened his eyes, everything was dark. He knew he was out of the tunnel only because someone was crying beside him.

"Josiah, wake up. Please, wake up," a soft voice was saying.

Josiah pulled a groggy hand to his face to wipe away something wet.

"Please, Josiah, wake up," the voice came again.

Only then, after his mind had cleared enough to listen closely, did he recognize the voice as his sister's. She was crouching over him where he lay. He realized, too, it was one of Hope's tears that had splashed on him.

"You're alive!" she cried. She leaned down and put her wet cheek next to his. "You're alive! You're alive!"

"You're alive, too," he said. He tried to smile, but it hurt. In fact, everything he did hurt. He struggled to sit up in the darkness, but between the pangs and aches everywhere he moved, and the fact that Hope wouldn't let go of him, he could shift only to a leaning position against something cold, hard, and damp.

He felt around gingerly. "Where are we?" he said.

"In a cave, I think," she said. She tried to sniff the tears out of her voice. "I don't know where. I was blindfolded when they brought me here, and on a horse, too."

"The Putnams?" he said. He knew he wasn't making sense yet, but the pieces just wouldn't come together. The last thing he remembered was Jonathon's fist coming toward his face. He touched the spot where the blow had landed and moaned.

"What is it?" Hope said.

"Jonathon got me a good one that last time."

She slid down beside him. "It's one thing to go to such great lengths to play this trick on us—it's another thing to hurt you," she said. "How could they think we wouldn't tell on them once we get out of here and get back to Salem Village?"

Josiah could hear the brave and confident tone coming back into Hope's voice. That was comforting. But then her last sentence clinked back into Josiah's mind, and he caught his breath. It wasn't right not to tell her. She had to have all the information—so she could start praying.

"You don't know, then?" Josiah said.

"Know what?"

"They don't think we'll ever get out of here, Hope," he said. "This isn't a trick. This is . . . this is the end."

Hope got to her feet and stood over him. "That blow to your head has taken away all your spirit!"

"It wasn't the blow to my head," Josiah said. "It's what they told me—Ann and Silas and the rest."

"Silas?" Hope said, crouching beside him. "What did Silas say?"

"He heard them all talking. They brought you here to leave you . . . to . . . to die."

She didn't say anything for so long that Josiah thought she might already have died—or at least fainted—right there in that squatting position beside him. But suddenly, he felt more than saw her toss her head back.

"It's obvious we're in a cave," she said. "We shall just make our way to the opening and find our way out."

"But—"

"Would you rather just sit here and let them have their way?" Hope said.

"No," Josiah said. He tottered painfully to his feet. "We can at least gather information, eh?"

"I don't care what you call it. Come on, let's go."

"Which way?" Josiah said.

Hope hesitated and then put her hands up on the cave wall. "I'm sure they brought me in from this direction, because when Jonathon pushed me to the ground, my hand hit on this big crack in the wall. I was facing just this way."

Josiah pictured Jonathon giving Hope a mighty shove, and he had to push his anger back into its place again. He had thought he'd burned it all out in the fight, but there always seemed to be plenty to spare.

Slowly, they made their way through the darkness, feeling along the damp wall with their hands.

"I remember this hole!" Hope shouted, as if she had found a nugget of gold. "We're going the right way!"

I pray we are, Josiah thought to himself. *Or we're going a long way in the wrong direction.*

It seemed as if they went on for hours. With each step, Josiah was more sure that the Putnams had never intended for them to be found. He was trying to ignore the nagging thought that maybe they never would be, when Hope squealed again.

"What is it?" Josiah said.

"A crack!" Hope said. "A big one. And I feel air coming through! This is where they brought me in, Josiah. I'm sure of it. Can't you smell that?"

Josiah fumbled for the crack and stuck his nose into it. He didn't smell anything but wet rock.

"It smells of the river," she said. She was crying again, but her voice was laughing. She pressed her nose against the crack and howled until Josiah was afraid she would lose control completely. "When you don't hear well, you have to count on other things to guide you," she said. "I remember this smell, because I was afraid they were going to throw me into the river. This is the opening, Josiah, and this crack must be—"

"Where the boulder is!" Josiah said. "The one they used to close off the entrance." He stood on his tiptoes to follow the crack up with his fingers until he couldn't reach it anymore. "Aye, that's what it is."

"So we've only to push this big stone out of the way and we're free!" Hope said. "Come on, Josiah! Push!"

They flattened themselves against the stone and shoved. Josiah had to chomp down on his lip to keep from howling in pain. But he pushed. And Hope pushed. But the boulder didn't move.

Hope's laughter died, and Josiah could hear her crying

softly as she slid down the boulder to the ground. Painfully, Josiah bent his knees and sat on his haunches beside her.

"Hope," he started to say.

But she coiled away from him and shrieked from some-place deep inside her.

"What was *that?*" she screamed.

"What? Hope, what's the matter?"

She couldn't answer him. She could only shake—so hard that Josiah thought she would crash her head against the rock.

"Stop it, Hope!" he cried. "Stop it now!"

"My foot!" she sobbed. "Something crawled across my foot! I can't bear this, Josiah!"

Josiah wasn't sure he could either, but the way she was shuddering and screaming frightened him more than just about anything else that had happened that whole terrifying day.

"Pull your feet up against you," Josiah said. "I'll find it. I'll find it and kill it."

Hope pulled herself into a sobbing ball, and Josiah peered around hopelessly. He could barely see the ground itself, much less anything crawling across it.

"Kill it, Josiah!" she kept crying. "I can't stand it."

Josiah searched the cave floor with his hands, but the only thing he found was a loose rock. His mind reeling, he snatched it up and smacked it against the ground. When it thudded, Hope stopped screaming.

"Did you get it?" she said.

"Aye," Josiah lied.

Hope began to breathe in huge gulping sobs, but at least she wasn't screaming anymore.

Forgive me, please, God, Josiah prayed. *I had to sneak this time.*

A tiny ripple of peace went through Josiah. It felt good to talk to God. Better than anything else he was doing in this cave anyway. He crept over next to Hope, who was twisted up like a spring and shaking all over.

"Hope," he said, "you have to listen to me."

"What are we going to do, Josiah?" she said. Her voice sounded on the edge of panic once more.

"We're going to pray," he said.

"No, Josiah, what are we going to *do?*"

"We're going to pray," he said again. "And you have to pray with me. Do it. Come on."

She didn't say anything, but he felt her bury her head in her arms. *All right, then*, he thought. *I'll pray for both of us.* He leaned his head back and looked toward the crack that separated them from the outside world. It was probably night-time, Josiah figured, so no light filtered in.

"God," Josiah said out loud. "We've gathered all the information we can. Whatever your will is for us, just let us know, and we'll do whatever you want."

"Please forgive me if my own stubbornness brought us here," a quavery voice joined in. "I meant no harm. I only meant to help, but you know that, and you know that Josiah doesn't deserve . . . this. We have no other help but you."

Josiah pulled his surprised eyes away from his sister and closed them. "And please, God," he said, "don't let us be afraid. I don't like to be afraid. It . . . it scares me."

"Amen," Hope said. And then, like the tinkling of some miracle bell, she began to laugh.

"What's so funny?" Josiah said. "You're worse than Abigail Williams, laughing at prayer!"

"Does she laugh at prayer?"

"Aye, I saw her just last Sunday in Meeting . . . but you didn't answer me. What was so funny?"

"You saying you didn't like to be afraid because it scares you. That's like saying you don't like pain because it hurts or you don't like starvation because it makes you hungry—"

"Could we talk about something else?" Josiah said uneasily.

"Ah, I might have known you'd be thinking of food," Hope said. Her voice was calm again, and he could almost feel the wheels of thought turning in her head.

"Did you discover that piece of bread I put in your whistle pouch the other day?" she said.

"Aye, and there's none of it left."

"Of course not."

"Ah!" Josiah said. He groped for the pouch that he had tucked inside his breeches at the sawmill—a hundred years ago now, it seemed—and yanked it open.

"You have food?" she said.

"No, but I have light. See if you can find any small sticks—anything that will burn. I think I can start a fire."

"With what?" she said.

"I have a knife and a piece of flint," he said, pulling them from the pouch.

"You can do that?" she said.

I hope so, he thought. "Gather some sticks."

"Where am I to find twigs in a cave?" she mumbled as she crawled away from him. "Perhaps a tree has sprouted up in here and dropped a few branches. . . ."

Josiah didn't hear the rest. His forehead was furrowed with worry and concentration as he scraped the knife across the flint. He didn't want to tell her that he had never been able to get a fire going this way. But he had seen Ezekiel do it just the other night. Then, after several attempts, a spark flew from beneath his hands.

"Hope!" he cried. "Get me anything. I've got a fire!"

"Here," she said. "Will this do?"

She thrust something that felt like a vine branch and some flowers into his hand. He didn't take the time to wonder what it was. He scraped his knife across the stone again and sparks appeared like tiny stars. In minutes, the vine Hope had handed him was sprouting little flames and a feeble light flickered against the walls of the cave. They both saw at once a scattering of small twigs and broken branches on the cave floor that they hadn't been able to see in the darkness.

"They must have blown in here during a storm," Hope said.

"Before that rock was rolled in front of it. Here, help me dig a trench 'round the fire."

It didn't take long for them to make a cozy fireplace, ringed by stones, that kept their fire burning merrily. The crack let in enough air to keep it going, and provided a place for the smoke to escape. Only when it was done did Josiah ask Hope, "What was that first thing you handed me?"

She shrugged and toyed with the tattered hem of her skirt. "'Twas a wreath I made out of a grapevine. I put some flowers on it and kept it in Joseph Putnam's woodshed. I wore it when . . . when Silas came."

Josiah could feel his face twisting. "Why?" he said.

She looked up at him from across the fire as if to answer, but the words faded from her lips, and she leaned forward. "Josiah!" she said. "It's a wonder you're not dead! If you could see yourself!"

Josiah put his hands up to his face and cringed. There was a huge lump on one cheek, and his nose felt twice its normal size. Then there was the pulsing pain in one arm and the burning from the scrape on the other.

"Did the Putnams do all that?" Hope said.

"Some of it," Josiah said. "I had an accident at the sawmill. But Silas took it worse than I did, I think."

Hope grunted and looked away. "I'm glad of that, then."

Josiah felt his eyebrows shooting up. "Why?" he said.

"Because he set up all of this, Josiah. It was a trap all along. I was a stupid girl to be fooled by him. He didn't even come to the woodshed this morning. It was Ann and Abigail who surprised me there. They tied me up, blindfolded me, threw me on a horse, and took me to another woodshed, where I lay until dinnertime when Jonathon and the others got there—still smelling of pigeon stew, I might add. They ate before coming to kill me! They're a rotten lot, the Putnams—and Silas, too! He may be the worst, for pretending to like me."

"He does like you," Josiah said. "It was he who got word to me that they'd done this. He was about to go with me to Joseph Putnam when Jonathon and Richard and Eleazer found us in the woodshed. He'd been waiting there for hours, Hope."

He could see her swallowing hard. "He . . . he was hurt by Jonathon, too, then?"

"Aye. The last time I saw him, he was still lying in the corner."

"This is wretched!" Hope cried. "This is horrible!" She grabbed her skirts in her arms and stood up. "We must get out of here, Josiah. We must go back and tell everyone everything. I don't care what they do to me either."

She marched toward the boulder, and once more Josiah painfully struggled to his feet. He hurt too much to do anything. *Perhaps we should just wait until Papa comes after us—*

But he stopped halfway through that thought. His father was in Salem Town. Papa probably wouldn't get home until late—or perhaps not until morning—and then how would he know where to find them? Even Silas didn't know, and why would Papa think to even ask Silas?

It was sure Silas wouldn't go to the Hutchinsons. If Jonathon hadn't beaten him to death, he was surely locked up in some Putnam cellar for being a traitor to the family.

Hope was right. If they were going to get out of there, they had to do it themselves.

She was scratching and clawing at the big rock, but Josiah picked up the largest branch that was waiting to be put on the fire.

"Papa always uses a lever when something is wedged," he said. "If I can pry this into the crack . . . "

The end of the branch was too big, so with shaking fingers, he whittled it to a point with his knife and stuck it in. Finally, he said, "Grab hold of the end and help me pull."

Hope did, and together they pulled until Josiah thought his eyeballs would pop out.

"This has to work," Hope said. "The Putnams got it open somehow to bring you in."

"Aye," Josiah said slowly. The truth crept in, and it wasn't friendly. "But they got it open from the outside," he said. "If we're to get it open from here, we have to push this boulder, and we can't."

"Do you know what I'm thinking, Josiah?" Hope said.

Josiah looked at her and almost laughed. Her hands were on her hips and her toe was tapping.

"I am thinking," she said, "that it is next door to impossible that the Putnam cousins thought of this all by themselves." She cocked an eyebrow at Josiah.

"You think their parents are part of this?" Josiah said.

"I wouldn't doubt it." She tossed the branch near the fire and sat down.

"Aye, that's truth," Josiah said as he sat down across from her. "Wait until I tell you what I saw on Giles Porter's desk today."

"What were you doing at Giles Porter's desk?" Hope said.

Josiah told her the story of his morning. When he got to the part about the sealed parchment papers, Hope's mouth fell open.

"I saw them just a few days ago on Reverend Parris's desk," Josiah said.

Hope nodded slowly. "So those must be the ones Reverend Parris claims were stolen from him. It would make more sense for Giles Porter to want them than the Putnams. At least that's one crime they didn't commit."

"Aye, but can you think how Papa is going to feel when he finds out Giles is doing sneaky things, when Papa told him he wanted no part of that? He's always believed in the Porters."

"I wonder if 'tis all of them, though," Hope said. "Perhaps it's just Giles."

Josiah's eyes sprang open. "I thought you liked Giles!"

Hope smiled mysteriously. "I only said he was handsome."

Josiah shook his head. "I'll never understand what difference that makes."

Hope crawled to his side of the fire and, to his amazement, snuggled up beside him and put her head on his shoulder. He was about to squirm away and ask her just what she thought she was doing when she said, "That's all right, Josiah. You're smart enough about other things. With you here beside me, I know we're going to get out of here alive. I feel a kind of . . . peace."

Josiah pawed around in his mind for words. "What kind of peace?" he said finally.

But she didn't answer. She was already asleep.

Chapter Fourteen

The crack of light that filtered into the cave around its stubborn stone door woke Josiah before Hope. She had slid down to a comfortable position with her head on his lap, but he'd spent the whole night propped against the boulder, and every part of his battered body ached. He felt like one of the eggs his mother often cooked—beaten in a bowl with a wooden spoon.

It made him sad to think of his mother. And it made him hungry to think of one of her eggs—as well as the bread, mush, or berries that were probably at this moment on the breakfast table beside them.

Probably not, Josiah thought. *She has probably been pacing around the house all night, crying, wringing her hands like pieces of laundry. . . .*

Josiah shook his head. Maybe it was better to think about food.

He slid carefully out from under Hope's sleeping head and stood up to take stock of his injuries. His arms and face were the things that hurt most. The rest of him was just stiff from the dampness in the cave and the strange bed he had spent the night on.

He could still squat, and he bent down to start the fire again—and then he saw it. Curled up on the other side of the tiny fireplace, it slowly raised its diamond-shaped head and rattled its tail in warning.

Josiah's mind flashed back to another encounter with a snake, on the edge of Edward Putnam's property. If it hadn't been for Joseph Putnam's quick thinking, he would have died that day. But this time Joseph Putnam wasn't there, and Josiah's heart began to thunder.

"Good morning," Hope said sleepily beside him. She tried to sit up, but Josiah put his arm out and pushed her down.

"Josiah, what on earth—?"

"Don't move!" he hissed at her.

The snake hissed, too, and rattled again, bringing up its head even more. Crazily, Joseph Putnam's words darted around in Josiah's head: "The old ones don't put all their venom into you. They know you're too big."

But this one was smaller than the rattler that had bitten Josiah before. If either of them were struck by this snake, it wouldn't matter what kind of boulder held them in the cave.

"What *is* it?" Hope whispered insistently.

Josiah knew she couldn't hear the hissing or the rattling. He tried not to move too much as he pointed to the snake. Her eyes widened, and she opened her mouth to scream.

Josiah tried to stop her. "Shhh!"

She plastered both hands over her mouth and froze beside him. Josiah wanted to do the same thing—just turn into a statue and wait for the snake to slither away. He was so frightened that he couldn't think of anything else to do.

But Hope, it seemed, was more frightened. A whimper escaped from her mouth, and like a stream bubbling up out of the ground, it burst suddenly into a scream.

"Kill it, Josiah!" she shrieked. "Kill it, please!"

"I don't know how!"

"Do what you did last night—when you killed that animal last night!"

Josiah's head spun. He hadn't killed anything last night. He'd only made her think he had.

The snake held its head up so far that Josiah didn't know how it was keeping its balance. A thin forked tongue lashed out, and Hope strangled another scream.

Slowly, hardly daring to move at all, Josiah reached out and felt for a rock. The snake watched with its tiny eyes, its tongue still whipping at the air. When Josiah felt a stone under his fingers, he picked it up and hurled it, as hard as he could with his good arm, toward the snake.

The rock hit it square in the face and bounced off behind it.

Standing to get a better look, Hope cried, "It's not dead!"

No, but it was flat on the ground for the moment. Before the snake could raise up again, Josiah moved closer, grabbed another, bigger rock, and smashed it down on the diamond-shaped head. The rattling and hissing stopped, and Josiah looked away. He was sure he was going to be sick.

Hope gasped for air. "Is it . . . dead?" she said.

Josiah nodded, though he made a wide curve around the snake's body to get to Hope. He sank down just before his knees gave way.

But Hope locked her hand around his arm and pulled him up again. "Josiah!" she cried. "We can't stay here. We can't stay another minute."

She lunged at the boulder blocking the cave's entrance and began to scratch and claw at it like a cat gone wild. He joined her until his hands were raw and Hope was pressed against the rock with no tears left to cry.

"Last night, I felt so hopeful," she said. "We prayed so hard, and I thought surely we would find a way."

"Aye," Josiah said.

They said nothing for a long time, and Josiah could hear Hope trying to get control of her breathing. Finally, she opened one eye and looked at him. "Is it still there?" she said.

"What?"

"That . . . thing."

Josiah looked over at the snake, motionless under the rock.

"Aye."

"You're sure 'tis dead?" she said.

Josiah nodded and looked at her curiously.

Hope tossed her curls and tilted her chin. "Well, if it didn't kill us, and it never will, God meant for us to get out of here alive, eh?"

Josiah wasn't sure he understood all that, but when it came to girls these days, he seldom understood much at all. Still, it was better to see her grasping at twigs of hope than crying and clawing at the wall.

"What's to be done with it?" she said, nodding toward the dead snake. "I don't think I can bear to look at it lying there."

"We could eat it," Josiah said suddenly.

"Oh, how wretched!"

"No, I've heard snake is as good as . . . well, that it tastes good."

"*You* eat it, then," she said. "I'd rather starve."

She watched with fascinated eyes as Josiah used his knife to skin the snake, cut it into bite-sized pieces, and poke them onto a stick. When the fire was blazing again, he held the stick over the tiny flames until juice began to drip and a pleasant smell floated up into the cave.

Hope wrinkled her nose as Josiah took the first bite, and she kept her eyes riveted on his face as he chewed.

"'Tis as they say?" she asked.

"Delicious," Josiah said, although he was sure the sole of his shoe would have tasted good right now, as hungry as he was.

She gave him one more long look before she took hold of a morsel and put it up to her mouth. "Isn't it poisonous?" she said.

"Nay, the Indians eat them all the time," Josiah said. "That's what Oneko told me once."

Hope closed her eyes and popped the meat into her mouth. She grinned at Josiah.

"Good?" he said.

"Good," she said. "But I sure am thirsty."

"Me, too," he said.

"Did Oneko teach you how to skin the snake like that?"

"Aye." Josiah chewed the snake meat thoughtfully.

The experiences with Oneko, the Indian boy, had happened to him so long ago that it was hard to believe they had happened at all.

"He was a handsome boy," Hope said.

Josiah groaned out loud.

"He was, Josiah! And you were such good friends. Do you miss him?"

"Aye."

"I miss the Widow Hooker," Hope said. She pulled another piece of snake meat from the stick and motioned for Josiah to take the last one. "You and she—and Oneko—saved my life." She watched the fire for a minute, and then looked back at her brother. "We've had so many strange and wonderful people in our lives this last year, don't you think?"

Josiah thought about that. "Oneko and the widow," he said.

"Our cousin Rebecca . . . and little Dorcas Carrier."

"Joseph Putnam and the Indian woman—"

Hope stared at him. "Indian woman!"

"Aye. Someday I shall tell you about her."

Hope nodded slowly. "Did she teach you anything?"

"It's sure she did."

"Each one of them has taught us something," Hope said.

Josiah felt an idea spring to life in his mind. "That's so we can gather information!" he said. "So we know what God's will is!"

Hope's eyes caught his excitement. "It's God's will that we get out of this cave, Josiah. I know it. Why else would you have been taught how to skin a snake? Why else would I have known to depend on my fingers since I can't depend on my ears? That's how we got to the right end of the cave." She settled happily into her skirts. "We shall be found, Josiah. I know it."

She looked so content to sit there and wait that Josiah didn't have the heart to disagree. But the thought of doing nothing while his father searched all of Essex County and beyond made his stomach churn uneasily.

"We still have to help," he said carefully.

She cocked her head at him.

"How would anyone passing by know we're in here?" he went on.

"Aye. We must give them a sign. You can write, Josiah." She stopped and frowned. "But we've nothing to write on . . . or with."

They sat in silence for a moment, and then Josiah opened his whistle pouch and pulled out the note he had gotten from Betty Parris.

"You could survive for a year on what you have in that pouch!" Hope said.

Josiah scowled. "'Tis too bad I wasn't carrying elderberry juice. We need it for ink."

"Or breakfast," Hope said, and then a moment later, her face brightened. "What about ashes, Josiah?"

"What about them?"

"Can you not use them for ink?"

Josiah picked up a piece of freshly charred wood and, turning the parchment over and spreading it on a rock, began to write in large letters.

"What does it say?" Hope asked.

"Help."

Hope shook her head. "You have always been a man of few words, Josiah," she said.

Josiah stood up with the sign and went to the crack that led to the outside. He slid the sign through and waited by the boulder.

Behind him, Hope chuckled softly. "Do you think someone is going to come running immediately?" she said.

He sat down by the fire again. "Nay. I thought I might hear if it fell or something."

"Do you remember when you used to stutter?" she said as he sat down by the fire again.

Josiah wiggled his shoulders. He would rather not think about it.

"I used to call you a brainless boy," she said.

"I was one."

"No!"

Josiah looked at her in surprise. Her black eyes were shining at him in the dim light.

"You never were," she said. "And you surely aren't now. You have saved me so many times, brother. You are better than anyone else who lives in that miserable village—you and Papa and Joseph Putnam."

Josiah scrambled up and went quickly to the crack. It wouldn't do for Hope to see him cry.

"So, what do you think has become of our sign?" he said. He hoped his voice didn't sound like tears.

"I don't know," she said. "But I think 'tis in God's hands now."

Josiah nodded and a peaceful feeling swept over him.

They talked until they could think of no more memories to take out and examine. Then Josiah found a piece of wood and started to whittle, while Hope picked up one of the flowers that had escaped the fire and began to pluck out its petals.

Josiah watched her for a minute. "Why are you doing that?" he asked.

She pulled out a petal. "He loves me." She pulled out another. "He loves me not. Whatever the last petal says tells me whether or not he loves me."

"Who?" Josiah said.

"I don't know! Someone . . . somewhere."

Josiah looked down at his toes and studied them for a minute. There was something he wanted to say, but just as surely as he was sitting here in this cave, it would come out limp and brainless. Still, he might never have another chance.

"Someone will!" he blurted out.

"What?"

"Someone will love you . . . because you're pretty and good and not silly like Rachel and Sarah and that spider Ann Putnam!"

Hope gazed at him, but she didn't laugh. Her eyes just shimmered. "Thank you, Josiah," she said softly.

There was a long silence as they both thought their own thoughts. Josiah built a small tower out of stones, and Hope drew pictures in the dirt with a stick.

"I don't know if I am good anymore," she said suddenly.

"Why?" Josiah said.

"I've been sneaky. I've done things behind Mama's and Papa's backs. I've made up my own mind what is good for me and what isn't." She sighed. "We wouldn't even be here if I was good."

Josiah just nodded. It was probably true. He knew that *he* certainly wouldn't be there if it wasn't for Hope.

"I don't like what's become of me either," he said. "I'm so angry all the time, and I want to fight. I want to hurt people because . . . I don't know why."

"Because they've hurt you," Hope said.

"But it's evil. I put my knee right in Jonathon Putnam's stomach. And I told Abigail that Reverend Parris loved his own daughter better than he did her, being adopted as she was."

"They probably deserved it," Hope said slyly.

"Then why do I feel . . . no better than that snake we ate?"

Hope looked at him as if she had just eaten something spoiled. "I know why," she said. "Because we're becoming like them."

Her words hit Josiah with a thud. "Aye," he said. "The Putnams must feel like this all the time."

"Perhaps they are the ones we should be praying for."

Josiah was sure he would have gotten down on his knees right then if he hadn't heard a sound outside the cave. He tilted his head to listen.

"What is it?" Hope said.

"I hear something!" he whispered. He crept to the crack and tried to see out, but the opening was too narrow. Only blinding sunlight hit his eye. With Hope clinging to his back as if she were trying to hear through him, he put his ear to the crack and listened again.

It was there—the sound—from far away but getting closer.

He opened his mouth to call out to it, but the words caught in his throat. It was hoofbeats he heard.

It was horses.

The Putnams' horses.

✠ ✠ ✠

Chapter Fifteen

ope squeezed the back of his arm.

"Do you hear someone coming?" she said. "What is it?"

"Horses," he said.

"Papa?"

Josiah turned to look at her. The same horror that he knew was in his eyes flashed through hers.

"Putnams," she said fiercely. "Come back to taunt us."

Or worse, Josiah thought gravely. He didn't have to say it. He was sure Hope had thought of it, too.

She yanked on his arm. "We must hide!"

Josiah's head was spinning, and he tried to latch on to a thought that made sense. "What if it *is* Papa or someone else come to rescue us and we're hidden back in the cave?" he said.

"But if it's the Putnams—"

"We can wait here and listen to who it is. It will take them some time to move this rock. If it's the Putnams, we'll still have time to hide."

Hope nodded.

"Just in case," he said, "destroy the fire so they won't know we've come this far."

She leaped behind him, and Josiah put his ear to the crack. The hoofbeats grew steadily nearer. There was more than one horse. Every Putnam had a horse. But so did almost everyone else in the village, Josiah reminded himself. *God*, he prayed with his eyes squeezed shut, *please let it be Papa*.

The horses drew so close that Josiah could at last hear voices, and he strained to make out whose they were. They were low-pitched voices that drifted toward him in bits and snatches.

"'Tis not Ann Putnam and Abigail!" Josiah whispered to Hope.

"Thank the Lord for that," she said as she joined him at the crack again.

Josiah put up his hand to quiet her. Outside, the hoof-beats had stopped, and he could hear footsteps crackling through underbrush and stomping across rocks. But there were no voices. No one spoke a word.

They're trying to sneak up on us, Josiah thought. He pressed his ear to the crack until the rock dug into his skin. *Please, someone say something, so we'll know whether to run for our lives*.

Just then a voice broke crisply into the silence. "It says we're to go this way."

"John Proctor?" Josiah said.

Hope nearly crawled up his back. "Mister Proctor!" she cried. "Mister Proctor, we're here! Help!"

Josiah called out, too, and found himself pushing the boulder as if the mere presence of John Proctor would make the rock easier to move. Through Hope's screams, he heard another voice, deep and commanding.

Josiah put his hand over Hope's mouth so he could hear.

"Josiah! Hope!" the voice said. "Hush now. We'll get you out of there!"

Hope tore Josiah's hand away and cried, "Papa!"

"Aye. Now get your wits about you, both of you, and help us."

Hope nodded and gasped for breath. Josiah clung to the rock and tried to stop his thoughts from flying in all directions. He had to concentrate on the task at hand.

"'Tis like the stone in front of Jesus' tomb," Papa said.

There was a pounding at the crack and John Proctor said, "Aye. Would that we had the angels here to roll it away. That's what it's going to take, Joseph."

Josiah put his mouth to the crack. "Papa?" he said. "We tried a lever, and I think 'twould have worked from out there."

"I think we found our angel," Papa said with a chuckle.

With Hope watching his face, Josiah listened while the two men tossed orders and suggestions back and forth. Both children had tears streaming down their faces.

"Those three young idiots never thought of this alone," John Proctor said.

"Aye," Papa agreed grimly.

Hope tugged at Josiah's now-tattered sleeve. "What are they doing? Will they be able to get us out?"

As if he had heard her, Papa called out, "Now then, you children, listen to me. We can drive wedges at top and side and roll this boulder just enough for one person at a time to slip out. You must be ready when I tell you."

Josiah tensed as he waited. He tried not to think of himself or Hope smashed like corn cakes between the rock and the cave wall. Hope curled her fingers around his wrist and didn't let go.

Above him, he heard hammering and watched as a piece of wood was inched into the crack. Farther down, another wedge appeared.

"Good, then," Papa called out. "Are you children ready?"

"Aye!" they answered.

"As soon as you see a space wide enough to squeeze through, you do it! You must move quickly."

Josiah nodded as if his father could see him and called back, "Aye, sir!"

The cave rumbled, and pebbles jarred loose from the crack and rained down on their heads. But Josiah didn't take his eyes off the crack.

Slowly, as if the sun were dawning, the sliver of light grew bigger—as wide as his hand . . . as wide as his leg . . . as wide as his body!

Josiah hurried toward the opening, and then he stopped.

"Go, Hope!" he cried. "You go first!"

But his sister only stared at the sunlight that streamed in on them and shook her head. "It isn't wide enough!" she said. "We'll be pressed to death!"

"Josiah! Hope! Come on!" the voices yelled from outside.

Hope shook her head. Josiah grabbed her shoulder and shoved her toward the opening. She tumbled through with him behind her.

Josiah wasn't on the ground for more than an instant

before he felt himself being hauled up and pulled against something hard and warm that smelled of his father. Despite Josiah's scraped and bruised face, Papa held him tight.

"Thank God," Papa kept saying into Josiah's hair. "Thank God."

Josiah blinked against the glaring sunlight and saw Hope's face close to his. They were both pushed against their father's chest, their breath almost squeezed out of them. Josiah closed his eyes again and let the tears come.

When Papa loosened his grip, the only person not crying was John Proctor, and even he smeared his sleeve across his eyes before he said, "'Tis a miracle."

Papa sank down onto a large rock and pulled Hope and Josiah against him again. *He thinks if he lets go of us, we'll be sucked back into the cave*, Josiah thought. Just in case he was right, Josiah hung on to his father's shirt as he hadn't done since he was five.

Hope pulled her face from Papa's neck. "It's my fault we're here, sir," she said. "Please don't punish Josiah."

Papa pushed her face against his chest. "I have no plan to punish anyone, child. I only want to thank God we found you."

"How *did* you find us?" Josiah said.

John Proctor reached inside his shirt and pulled out a piece of parchment. He crouched down and spread it on his knee for them to see. Josiah stared. It was a map, labeled in the round, neat handwriting of Betty Parris.

"We're past Boxford," Papa pointed out. "We would never have thought to look this far without a map. 'Twas under the knocker on the front door when I came home from Salem Town this morning."

"We came near to not following it," John Proctor said. "Thought it was the work of the Putnams sure."

Papa looked straight at Hope. "But your mother said we should ask Silas Putnam, that Josiah said you met with him, and that he could be trusted."

Hope swallowed hard and nodded. "That's true, Papa."

"Aye, it is," he said briskly. "Joseph Putnam discovered him in his woodshed, being nursed by Tituba. He looked as if he'd been trampled by a herd of horses. Silas said he only knew his cousins had taken you both, but he knew not where. He said Betty Parris had drawn the map, probably from what she heard from Abigail." He shook his head and looked up at John Proctor. "The children have woven a web as tangled as ours, eh?"

John Proctor nodded. "And I fear we are all captured in it."

"Ah, but we found you, eh?" Papa squeezed them once more. "God gave us a sign that we were close when we found your message."

Josiah lifted his face to see John Proctor holding up the parchment with its ashen "Help" smeared across it.

"I have smart children, John Proctor," Papa said. "God be praised for that." He held them for a moment longer, and then stood up, steadying them both with his big hands. "We must get back to the village. Your mother is well nigh dead with worry." He laughed softly. "Except that she has Constance Putnam to keep her mind busy." He looked up at the sky. "Before the day is out, it's sure there will be a new Putnam."

"I pray 'tis a good one," John Proctor said.

It was well into the afternoon when Josiah teetered unsteadily across Joseph Putnam's yard to meet his mother.

She took both her children into her arms with almost as much fierce strength as her husband had.

"God is merciful," she said as she stroked their hair and studied their faces with her soft eyes. "He took care of you."

"God took care of Josiah, and Josiah took care of me," Hope said.

"And now you must take care of Josiah," Mama said. She brushed her finger gently over Josiah's swollen and bruised face.

As their mother went back to Constance Putnam, Hope took Josiah's hand and led him into Joseph Putnam's big kitchen.

"Sit you here while I fetch some water," she said.

Josiah laughed to himself as he watched her snatch a pail and rush out the back door. She was going to take care of him? She looked as if she had been in a fight with a bear cub all night—and lost. He really didn't want anyone to fuss over him. Wearily, he put his head down on the table. He just wanted to sleep.

"Captain!"

Josiah lifted his head to look at Joseph Putnam, and this time he laughed out loud. Joseph's hair was poking up like porcupine quills, and his collar stuck out at rakish angles from his shirt. He was the spitting image of a big, confused bird about to take flight.

"Aye, I'm laughing, too!" Joseph said. "My favorite captain has returned from his kidnapping and a baby is about to be born!" Joseph glanced anxiously at the ceiling. "Right up there in that room, though not as quickly as I would like." He scooted a chair close to Josiah and straddled it. "It takes a long time for a baby to make its way into this world, did you know that?"

Josiah didn't, nor did he want to. But he needn't have worried. Just as quickly as he had sat down, Joseph Putnam stood up again and began to tread back and forth across the kitchen, hands raking through the porcupine quills.

"Your mother is an angel," he said. "Constance is quite calm with Deborah at her side." He stopped and grinned sheepishly at Josiah. "Perhaps I'm the one who needs Deborah, eh?"

Josiah grinned.

"Joseph," said Josiah's father from the doorway. "John and I must go to Ezekiel Cheever to see to this business." A flicker of a smile passed across his face. "You'll be all right until I return?"

"Aye! Of course. I have the captain here to nurse me along." He looked at Josiah, and then back at Papa. "You're going to have them arrested then, eh?"

Papa nodded sadly. "Aye. Though I fear it's their fathers who ought to be put in the stocks . . . and they never will."

"Perhaps this is a start toward the end of all this, though, Joseph," young Putnam said. He put his hand on Papa's shoulder. "Someday, God willing, my brothers will see how far they've gone astray. You're surely pushing them in that direction."

Papa nodded and looked at Josiah. "As soon as your sister has washed those wounds, get you to bed, both of you. We'll stay here at Joseph's for the night. We all need each other's friendship now."

He stepped out of the room, and Hope strode in with a pail of water and a rag, which she briskly applied to Josiah's face while he yowled.

"You're making more fuss than Constance," Joseph Putnam said, eyes twinkling. And then he jolted from his seat. "I must see to her!" he cried and bolted from the room.

Josiah shook his head. Some things he was sure he would never understand.

When Josiah was washed, bandaged, and poulticed until he felt like a kneaded lump of dough, he crawled into the bed he had been in for his snakebite. He looked drowsily out the window as the sun sank behind the village. He was asleep in moments.

Once, he was awakened by voices outside his door—his father's and Joseph Putnam's.

"Thomas Putnam is on fire with anger," he heard his father say.

"Of course," Joseph said. "His son and nephews are shut up at Ingersoll's Inn like prisoners."

"They're to be taken to Salem Town again for trial, though it didn't do much good last time, did it?"

"They didn't try to commit murder last time," Joseph Putnam said.

A chill went through Josiah, but he pulled the quilt around him to send it away. It didn't matter for the moment. For now, he was safe and his mind wasn't knotted up with questions and anger. He smiled to himself. Papa had been right. There was a peace that came from doing God's will.

It was dark the next time he woke up. This time, he heard an unfamiliar sound. He listened, and then sat straight up in bed.

It was a baby crying.

He slipped from under the quilt and padded silently across the plank floor to the door. A candle flickered on a table in the hall, and beside it stood Joseph Putnam, holding something in his arms as if he were afraid it would break.

He looked up and smiled through the candlelight at Josiah.

"Come here, Captain," he said. "You'll want to welcome my son aboard, eh?"

Josiah felt like he had to tiptoe as he crossed the hall. The rush of the afternoon had settled into a peaceful silence he didn't want to disturb. It was as if everyone in the house—perhaps in the world—was sleeping except him, Joseph, and the tiny wrinkled form Joseph held out in front of him.

"Do you want to hold him?" Joseph said.

Josiah took a step backward.

"I'll tell you a secret, Captain," Joseph said. "I, too, thought he'd be crumpled if I touched him, but he's strong as a colt, just like his namesake."

Josiah looked up from the baby to Joseph.

"Daniel Josiah Putnam," Joseph said. "I think you'd better have a talk with him."

Josiah couldn't explain why his chest suddenly puffed up as he stuck out his arms and curled them around the warm bundle Joseph put into them. He was surprised how sturdy the baby felt and how much his face looked like that of a wise little old man.

"He looks like he knows things," Josiah said.

"Aye, it's sure he does. And the rest you'll have to help me teach him, eh?"

Josiah studied the baby. "May I . . . may I touch him?" he said.

"Aye, I think he's waiting for that."

Josiah hitched the baby up in his good arm and put a shy finger on the baby's hand. At once, the tiny fingers wrapped themselves around Josiah's finger and held on.

"He is strong!" Josiah said.

"Aye. I told you!"

Not to be left out of the conversation, Daniel Josiah Putnam opened his mouth and let out what sounded to Josiah like the beginning of a squall. He looked nervously at Joseph, who looked back just as nervously.

Mama came out of a room down the hall and glided toward them with her arms held out. "This young man is wanting his first breakfast," she said, smiling shyly. "I don't think you want to wait until he starts demanding it."

Josiah gratefully handed over the baby.

"Captain, what say you to a cup of cider to celebrate?" Joseph said, clapping him on the shoulder. "Your papa's waiting for me on the porch."

Papa was gripping the arms of a chair and peering hard at the stars when Joseph and Josiah joined him with three mugs of cider.

"Those are hard thoughts you're thinking," Joseph Putnam said.

"Ach," Papa said, "and too hard for this night, when there is so much to be thankful for, eh?"

He held up his mug, and Josiah and Joseph held up theirs. Josiah waited a minute before he drank. He was feeling like one of the men, and he wanted to savor that.

"So you have a son to raise," Papa said to Joseph.

"Aye, and I shall stay in Salem Village and raise him here. I hope you'll be here to show me how, Joseph."

Josiah looked sharply at his father. He had never heard that his father had any plans to do otherwise.

"I know not, Joseph," Papa said. "I know not. I fear the people have forgotten what our fathers came to this wilderness to see. I think perhaps 'tis time to find a new wilderness—one where God reigns, not jealous, frightened men."

"But my good man," Joseph said, leaning forward to look into Papa's face, "surely after what has happened to Josiah and Hope, the Putnams will see what it has come to. They will listen to you now, and if Reverend Parris is truly the servant of the Lord, he will lead them in that."

Josiah watched his father, and his mind began to spin again. Just when he had found peace, Papa was stirring up the waters. *Leave Salem Village?* Josiah thought. *The only home I've ever known?*

"I would like to believe that, Joseph," Papa said. "Old Israel Porter convinced me that that was true. I always thought that with the men God gave me to fight on my side— you, Joseph, and the Porters—we could turn the church of Salem around. . . ."

But he didn't go on, because out of the darkness came the sound of hoofbeats. All three heads turned as a voice called from horseback.

"Are you yet a father, Joseph Putnam?" cried Giles Porter. "And my sister a mother?"

Josiah felt himself turning to wood as Giles jumped from his horse and strode up the front steps. Joseph Putnam stood up to greet him, and Josiah could see the stiffness in his neck, too. Josiah didn't dare look at his father. There was still one thing he hadn't told him.

"Aye, and you're an uncle," Joseph Putnam said politely. "It's a nephew you have."

Daniel *Josiah*, Josiah wanted to point out to Giles. But he kept his mouth shut.

"Let's see the lad!" Giles said. "After all, he's half Porter, eh?"

As Joseph led Giles into the house, Josiah heard his father sigh heavily beside him.

"May God have mercy on the child's soul for that," he said.

"Amen," Josiah whispered.

Chapter Sixteen

There was no more talk of leaving Salem Village as the Hutchinsons left for home at daylight. Josiah didn't dare ask, for fear of what his father might tell him. And the way his father worked at the morning chores, Josiah was sure Papa was as attached to his land as ever.

"We've much work to catch up on, Josiah," Papa said. "We must water the animals, clean the barn, and walk the fields to check on the crops. The sawmill can wait a day or two while we see to the farm."

Josiah and his father carried their tools into the field and began to work. It had been a long time since he and his father had worked side by side on the land, and Josiah felt peace creeping back in again, like the warmth of a fire after a cold day outside. Even in the stifling heat of the Massachusetts afternoon, he was grateful for that warmth.

Only one thing clouded his sunny thoughts—the picture

in his mind of the parchments with their blue wax P's on Giles
Porter's desk. He had to tell his father. Papa needed all the
information, especially now.

I don't want to leave Salem Village, he thought. *If Papa
doesn't know how sly Giles Porter really is, perhaps he won't
be so anxious to leave.*

Josiah slashed at a weed with his hoe, and then leaned on
the handle. He had done enough hiding of things already.
Papa had to see for himself what God's will was. Letting the
hoe drop to the dirt, he went toward the row of corn near the
road where his father was working. But his heart sank. There,
leaning down from his horse and shaking his fist, was Thomas
Putnam.

Josiah hung back and waited, and Papa turned slightly to
acknowledge his presence.

"I shall follow Cheever's wagon to Salem Town!" Thomas
Putnam was shouting. "I'll see to it that he and Willard don't
mistreat my son and my nephews!"

"The way they mistreated my children?" Papa said quietly.
"They meant to leave them there to die, Thomas, and I am
not so sure they did it on their own. I hope you and God will
forgive me if I care not how those boys are treated."

"Your children will have to testify in court to the way they
were treated!" Thomas Putnam cried, his red face oozing
sweat.

"Aye," Papa said. "I know that." He looked over his shoulder and beckoned to Josiah with his hand. "And my children
know that."

"Does your daughter know that I shall bring in a Boston
lawyer? Does she know that he will expose her for luring in

my nephew Silas like an evil temptress? Does she know he will prove that Richard and the others were only trying to protect their cousin from sin?"

Something exploded from Papa's chest. Josiah backed up three steps before he realized the explosion was laughter.

"You'll not find it funny when your daughter is in the witness chair!" Thomas shouted. He had worked himself into a lather now, and perspiration ran in torrents from his forehead and down his chin. Josiah saw a shower of it fly out behind the man as he took off on his horse, shouting over his shoulder, "I shall see you Hutchinsons in court!"

Papa's laughter died with the retreating hoofbeats, and he looked solemnly at Josiah. "I think it's time this family had a talk," he said. "Fetch your sister into the house."

There was no peace in Josiah's heart when he called to Hope in the vegetable garden and told her about the family meeting.

But she wiped her hands on her apron and stood up, chin tilted. "We knew it was coming," she said. "And we have naught to be afraid of. We must be honest."

"Aye, but do you know that Papa is thinking about leaving Salem Village, and us with him?"

Hope squeaked open the gate and stepped out next to her brother. "If that is what he wants to do, that is what he will do," Hope said. "I've learned one thing from this, Josiah, and that is not to try to skirt what Papa knows is best." She stuck out her elbow. "Come along, then," she said.

Josiah looked quizzically at her arm.

"Take hold, foolish boy, and let us go in together."

Awkwardly, Josiah hooked his elbow through hers. Girls!

But when they entered the kitchen and saw Papa gripping the arms of his chair, he hated to let go.

"Deborah, sit you here," Papa said. He motioned his wife to a chair next to his. "Josiah, Hope, pull those chairs in close. We have hard business to discuss, and we must do it as one."

Everything seemed to slow down to an unnatural pace as Josiah dragged a chair close to his father and sat. Even Papa's eyes moved slowly, searching each of their faces before he began.

"I have worked long and hard to try to bring God back into this village so that we may live in the peace of His love. I have tried everything I know. I took leave of the church and went to Salem Town. Next, I plunged myself into my business ventures and ignored my fellow villagers. Then I came back to the church here and prayed for it from within. Through it all, I— and all of us—have been pulled further and further down by the people who seem to resist the Lord's very presence. I thought I could bring those people together and make them see what crimes we were all committing against our neighbors, but that, too, has failed. I see only one chance left now, and that is to see that the young men who threaten to carry on this tradition of hatred are locked away—forever if need be—so that we may start fresh. Do you understand me, all of you?"

Three heads nodded. It seemed wrong to speak when Papa's strong, wise words had already filled the room.

"I must know if you are willing to fight this last fight with me," he went on.

They started to nod again, but Papa put up his hand. "You must know what that means, and you must be honest with me."

I know what you mean, Josiah thought. *You need all the information so you can know what God's will is.*

"Hope," Papa said.

Josiah's heart lurched, and he could only imagine how Hope felt inside.

"Aye, Papa," she said. Her voice didn't waver.

"In this fight, Thomas Putnam intends to accuse you of being some 'evil temptress' for Silas Putnam. I know that you met with the boy. Josiah has already told us that, and we are all thankful that he did." Joseph Hutchinson leaned his mighty forearms on his thighs and looked hard into Hope's eyes. "But I must know why, Hope. I must know why you slipped away to be alone with a boy."

He was keeping his voice even, but Josiah could hear the other questions fighting to be asked. He imagined his father also thinking, *Why did you do this when you know it is against my wishes and the rules of our faith for you to meet with a boy—any boy—alone? And why the son of one of my enemies?*

But those questions didn't come, and Papa waited silently for Hope to answer. She looked back into his piercing blue eyes with her own dark ones. They were frightened, but they were brave.

"Silas came to me after what happened last spring," she said, "and he told me that he hated what his cousins had done and that he was sorry they had frightened me. He was kind and I . . . I wanted to find out if he was really as good as he appeared to be. He invited me to come to the farm sometimes when he was working." Her eyes pleaded with her father. "I know it was wrong, but I was afraid you would forbid me, and I wanted to so much because I thought if I could discover that he was a good Putnam, that could be a help to you." Tears threatened at the edge of Hope's voice. "Please, Papa, please believe me. When Josiah helped me to meet with Silas in Joseph Putnam's woodshed, it was only so we wouldn't be seen by Silas's cousins. We did nothing except talk." Two tears spilled over, but she didn't take her eyes from her father's face. "I have given you no reason to trust me, Papa. I put Josiah in danger. I was willful and stubborn. We both almost died because I went against your wishes, but I ask you to please believe me."

She couldn't say any more because the tears took over her voice. Josiah wanted to pat her back—or do something to comfort her—but his hands lay in his lap like stones. Joseph Hutchinson nodded to his wife, and Deborah went to Hope and put her arm around her shoulders. Josiah sighed. Good, then. *Somebody* was comforting her.

Everyone was quiet while Hope cried. Then Papa sat back in his chair. "Hope," he said, "look at me."

Her face lined with tears, she lifted her chin.

"I believe you," he said, "and I forgive you. You've learned a hard lesson, one I know you'll not soon forget."

"Never," she said.

"We Puritans have always said that there are no excuses for doing wrong, only forgiveness," Papa went on. He ran his hand slowly across the back of his neck. "But I think many times there are reasons for our sinning. It's sure Reverend Parris would not agree, but I know . . . I know that the foolish things both of you have done this past year are owed to the hate that has taken hold in this town. You must know that."

Papa leaned forward—and so did the children—and continued speaking. "If I see that this same hate cannot be brought down in the fight we have ahead, I will give up the fight. I think I will know then that it is God's will that we leave this place."

Something grabbed at Josiah's chest, and he put his hand up to stop it. But the pain was coming from the inside, and Josiah could only let it ache as he listened.

"I have talked to Phillip English. We might do well to go to the Virginia Colony, where I can work as his partner and expand our shipping business in the South." He tried to smile. "You would like that, eh, Josiah, with your love of ships and the sea?"

Josiah wanted to shake his head and shout, *No, I would hate it! What of William and Ezekiel and Joseph Putnam? What of the farm and the river and the Blessing Place? What of all that?*

Papa was watching his face. Josiah bit his lip and nodded, but he knew his father wasn't fooled. Joseph Hutchinson looked away and stood up.

"Good, then," he said. "Now we have naught to do but pray on it. Deborah, some supper, eh?"

The air was smothery hot as Josiah lay in his bed that night, wide awake and tortured with thoughts. He was sure no one else was sleeping either, especially Hope. He could hear her behind her curtains, sighing, and flopping about like a fish.

"I don't want to leave Salem," he whispered to her.

"Nor do I," Hope said. She pulled the curtain aside to

look at him with tear-filled eyes. "I've never done so much crying," she said. "I'm as much a baby as Daniel Josiah."

She slipped from her bed, and Josiah scooted over on the cot. She pulled her knees up under her nightdress as she sat to face him.

"You know what I know, don't you?" she said.

"What?"

"That sending Richard, Jonathon, and Eleazer away forever isn't going to change things. The problem is with their fathers, Josiah, and you know it."

Josiah did, but he refused to nod his head. It seemed the minute he let himself believe it, they would be on their way to Virginia, with Salem Village far behind them.

"Are you angry with Papa?" she said.

Josiah looked at her in surprise. "No! Are you?"

She shook her head. "No. I only hope I can be as true to God's will as he is."

Josiah got out of bed and went to the chest under the window. Hope padded after him.

"What is it you see when you sit here so many nights?" she said.

Josiah looked down on the village, resting peacefully in the summer night, hiding all its hatred and evil plans inside its clapboard houses, hiding them from everyone but . . .

"God," Josiah said.

Hope looked over his shoulder. "You see God?"

"I try to find Him, anyway."

"And do you?" she said.

Josiah looked out again. Instead of the houses, the farms, and the narrow dirt road that led toward the sawmill, he saw pictures of himself at this window asking for help. And always, somehow, finding it.

"Aye," he said. "I always do."

Hope was quiet for a moment, and then she laughed softly. "I believe you," she said. "But it's sure that isn't God coming toward us now."

They both leaned out the window to peer at the figure that rounded the oak tree and ran across their yard.

"That's Ezekiel Porter!" she said. "What is he up to? Some foolish plan, I'm sure!"

But the face that turned up to them wasn't full of adventure. It was full of panic.

"Josiah!" he cried. "Get your father! The sawmill—it's on fire!"

The reflection on the Frost Fish River looked like sunrise as Josiah and his father tore across the Ipswich Road. The crashing of the flames was deafening, and they had to shout to be heard by Giles and Benjamin.

"We need more buckets!"

"We'll form a brigade from the river!"

"The wheel's gone, but we can save the housing!"

But Joseph Hutchinson looked up at the angry mass of smoke and blazing wood and shook his head.

"Joseph! We can save it!" Giles shouted.

"We can put out the fire, but the mill's gone! You know it, Giles! It's gone!"

More buckets were brought, and Josiah and Ezekiel joined the line of neighbors who formed a chain from the river to douse the flames and keep the fire from spreading to

the nearby farms. But Josiah didn't feel like a hero as he
dunked pail after pail into the Frost Fish River, eyes streaming, coughing against the thick smoke that choked the air. He
knew there would be nothing left but a pile of black rubble
when they were through. They weren't saving anything.

"We must talk of rebuilding," Benjamin Porter said. "But
tomorrow is soon enough. Prudence, more cider, eh, for these
parched throats?"

They sat in the Porter kitchen around the table, Josiah
and Ezekiel, Benjamin and Giles, and Joseph Hutchinson.
Prudence set another pitcher of cider on the table, but only
Giles reached for it.

"Come on, now, lads," Giles said. His face was black with
soot and striped with sweat, but he still smiled his charming
smile. "We've lost a good deal, but I have good news about
other things that may sweeten this vinegar for us. I think this
night is a good time to share it, eh?"

Josiah rolled his eyes and looked at his father. Joseph
Hutchinson sat staring. His face, his shoulders, even the
powerful hands that circled his mug looked beaten.

"Do y'think the fire was set, Benjamin?" Papa said, as if
Giles had never spoken.

Benjamin Porter's eyes shifted, but he had to nod. "Aye. I
found torches at every corner."

Papa's thick eyebrows gave a jerk. "We can't blame the
Putnam boys for this one. They're in the Salem Town jail
tonight."

But we can blame their fathers, Josiah thought. The pain
in his chest wrenched again. If his father couldn't win his fight

by putting the young Putnam boys away, he couldn't win it at all. Salem Village would soon be no more than a memory for the Hutchinsons.

"Putnams! Parris! What does it matter?" Giles said. "If you gentlemen will listen to me, I have news."

"What news, Giles?" Papa said wearily. "Tell it so I can go home to bed."

Giles stood at the head of the table, as if he were about to reveal some great mystery. Josiah looked at Ezekiel. His friend was hanging on his cousin's every word.

Giles's gray Porter eyes shone. "We may be rid of Reverend Parris sooner than we dreamed. Rumor has it that Parris was called under false pretenses—"

"Meaning?" Papa barked.

"Meaning he was promised things here that no one had the right to promise him and that there are things in his past that would have prevented his being called to this church if anyone had known." Giles folded his hands over his stomach and looked at the others importantly. "Things like a business of his that failed because he mismanaged the money. His being driven from Barbados for—"

"How do you know all this, Giles?" Papa said sharply.

Josiah began to gnaw on his lip.

"It is said," Giles went on, with his eyes shining, "that it is all in those documents Parris claims were stolen from the study in the parsonage."

"Why would he bring attention to the documents that would destroy him?" Benjamin Porter said.

"They say at Ingersoll's Inn that Parris claims the documents reveal just the opposite, and someone took them so they could make them look as if he were guilty of all those things."

"That is too complicated to be true," Papa said.

"Of course it is," Giles said—too cheerfully. "People were beginning to ask to see the documents, so Parris probably destroyed the papers himself, then claimed they were stolen. Everyone has accepted that and stopped demanding to see them."

Joseph Hutchinson pushed back his chair and stood up, his big hands flat on the table as he glared into Giles's eyes.

"Do you accept that, Giles?" Papa said.

Giles's smile came as expectedly as a cat's meow when it's squeezed. "Certainly not," he said.

"Why?"

"Because I know Parris. We all know Parris. And we all know the Putnams are a part of it. We have only to keep asking them about these papers, and they will trip over themselves somewhere and expose the truth."

"And what is the truth, Giles?" Papa asked. "Surely you know."

The smile on Giles's face faded. "I've told you what I know."

"Have you?"

"Joseph, I—"

"Have you? Do you know what really happened to those papers? Did you have anything to do with it, Giles?"

By now, Josiah's lips were raw from biting them. *Please, Giles, tell the truth*, he wanted to scream. *Be a man and tell the truth. I don't want to be the one who has to tell my father!*

But Giles was looking hard at Papa, and there was no charming smile on his face. His eyes glittered.

"Are you accusing me of wrongdoing, Joseph?"

"I am asking questions to which I must have honest answers, once and for all, Giles," Papa said. "I must have them. I have important decisions to make for my family now, and I must have the truth so I can know what God's will is for us."

"I know only what I have told you, and I resent your accusing me—"

Papa slammed his hand down on the table. "My children are more honest with me than you are, Giles Porter. A grown man and you cannot own up to your—"

Suddenly, a meek voice interrupted. "Look on his desk, Papa."

All eyes snapped to Josiah. His father took hold of his shoulder and pulled him to his feet.

"What is this about, son?"

Josiah pointed to the table in the corner where the stacks of papers still sat as they had two days ago, before the whole world had changed.

"I think the papers you want are there on the table," Josiah said.

Papa let go of his shoulder and stalked toward the table. Giles scrambled after him like a guilty child.

"Those are my personal papers, Joseph!" he protested.

Papa scattered them with one hand and picked up a parchment bundle, sealed with blue wax. Josiah held his breath.

"For your sake, Giles," Papa said quietly, "I hope this P stands for Porter."

Giles froze with his grabbing hand hanging useless in the air as Papa broke the seal and scanned the document with his eyes. Slowly, silently, he folded it and put it, with the others, inside his smoke-stained shirt.

"Why, Giles?" he said.

"I wonder that you would ask such a question," Giles said stiffly. "After Reverend Parris attacked you in his sermon, I thought to have revenge. Would you not do the same for me?"

"No," Papa said, "because I will not stoop to the level of the Putnams, and I didn't want to believe that you would either. Tell me, Giles," he went on in a voice that frosted the room, "did you have aught to do with the damage to Reverend Parris's wagon as well?"

Josiah didn't give Giles a chance this time. The pain in his father's eyes was more than he could stand.

"It's sure he did, Papa," Josiah said. "When I was home with the snakebite, I saw him from our window, coming from the Parrises' barn."

Giles spat out a laugh. "Why is it the boy comes up with all this 'evidence' now? Why did he not come forward sooner?"

Papa looked at Josiah with the same question on his face.

"Because I knew it would cause you pain, sir," Josiah said to his father. "Because the Porters are our friends."

Giles looked at the ceiling with his lips tightly pursed. Prudence flattened herself against the fireplace wall, and Benjamin stared deep into his mug of cider. If he hadn't known it before, Josiah knew now what shame looked like.

The only person he couldn't look at was Ezekiel. Ezekiel could be sneaky, and he had been a coward once. But he had proven his bravery. Josiah didn't want to see him ducking his head over something Josiah was sure he had known nothing about.

Papa split the silence with his deep, clear voice. "Ach, Giles," he said. "Do you not see what you have done? Not only have you brought sorrow on these innocent people—your own family—but you have become part of a tangled web here in this village that I fear none of you will be able to break free from."

Josiah thought he looked sadder than he had ever seen. Sadder than when Hope had been sick. Sadder than when old Israel had died. So sad that Josiah had to blink back his own tears as he watched him say his next words.

"As for me and mine," Papa said, "we will not live with our souls enmeshed in hatred and lies. I leave you to it . . . and I pray for you."

So it's done, Josiah thought numbly as he followed his father away from the Porters' silent house. Papa had collected the information and prayed that God's will would be made known. It had, and he had made a decision. *But is there peace?* Josiah wondered as he watched the lines in his father's face grow ever deeper.

☦ ⸭ ☦

Chapter Seventeen

Standing in the doorway of the Hutchinson kitchen, Josiah decided the room looked as empty as he felt inside.

The long, plank table where he had eaten hundreds of bowls of mush was packed in the wagon outside with Hope's spinning wheel and the barrels stuffed with Mama's pewter plates and wooden trenchers. The floor had been sanded to a shine, and the fireplace was swept clean and scrubbed, waiting for Francis Nurse's grandson and his new wife to come in and build their first fire. Even the diamond-shaped panes in the windows, which had always flickered like happy faces in the firelight, glared back at him like vacant eyes.

For weeks, he had been thinking how much he would hate to leave this friendly room—the room where he had helped nurse Hope back to health, showed his family that he had learned to read, listened to his father and Joseph

172

Putnam talk of important things. . . .

But now, without a pot of his mother's stew bubbling over the fire or Hope stitching a quilt by the window or his father gripping the arms of his chair, Josiah didn't want to be here at all. He was glad to escape when Hope called from the yard, "Josiah! They're coming!"

As he dashed out through the hall, he didn't look into the now-hollow best room, whose family Bible and pewter inkwell had been packed into the barrels with the other things. Every lifeless room he went into only made his chest ache more.

"William and Sarah are already in the barn," Hope said to him. "I'm going to fetch Betty Parris."

"What about Ezekiel and Rachel?"

Hope shrugged. "Betty sent them word. Perhaps she can tell us if they're coming."

Josiah dragged the toes of his boots as he went toward the barn. He was in no hurry to get to the last meeting of the Merry Band—especially if Ezekiel didn't come. They hadn't seen each other since that awful night in the Porters' kitchen. Even though Giles had returned the papers to Samuel Parris, there was a blotch on the Porter name now. Josiah had decided Ezekiel must be pretty angry with him for telling on Giles.

Things didn't brighten much when he got to the barn. Sarah was already sniffling. "I know we shall never see you and Hope again," she said tearfully.

"I told you if you were going to blubber all night you shouldn't come," William said. But his own face was as long as an evening shadow.

Josiah dropped down on the bare floor, strangely smooth

without its usual piles of hay. The animals had all been sold, and although Josiah was happy that his favorite cow, Ninny, was grazing in William's pasture, it was hard to be here without the smell of the oxen and the gentle stamping of the horse.

"Now this is a cheerful group," Hope said from the doorway. She crossed the barn with Betty in tow and put her hands on her hips. "There will be no tears and heavy faces tonight, ladies and gentlemen," she said. "This is a celebration. The Hutchinsons are going off on a new adventure."

That had been Hope's attitude ever since it was finally decided that they were moving to Virginia. She was more excited than Josiah about boarding all their belongings onto one of Phillip English's ships and sailing down the coast. At first, Josiah had thought she was only trying to put up a brave front for Papa, but even now her black eyes sparkled with all she had ahead. Josiah wished he could feel that way.

Hope settled herself down next to Sarah and took her arm. Betty slid in next to Josiah and looked bashfully at everyone.

"I can't stay long," she whispered to Josiah. "Tituba is keeping watch for me."

"Aye," Hope said. "If we hear an owl hooting, we're to send her home at once."

William's eyes widened. "Tituba can make an owl hoot?"

Josiah snorted. "No, ninny! She can make a sound like an owl!"

Sarah sent up a chorus of giggles, and Josiah had to chuckle with her. William was a simpleton sometimes—but it felt good to laugh. They were all howling when the barn door creaked open and a pair of pointy cheekbones poked in.

"Ezekiel!" Hope cried. "Is Rachel—?"

Rachel Porter slid in behind him, and both Porters ran to join the group. Josiah held his breath.

Ezekiel sat down on the other side of him and punched his arm. Josiah broke into a grin. He didn't have to leave Salem Village with Ezekiel mad at him.

"We're all here," Hope said. "The Merry Band." She beamed at all of them until William and Ezekiel started studying their boot tops, faces red, and the girls' eyes brimmed with tears. Josiah didn't know which to do—cry or look awkwardly at his feet—so he did neither.

"I have an idea," he said.

"Good, then," William said. "You always have the best ones."

"What say you if we each tell the best thing we remember about the Merry Band?"

They looked at each other for a moment, and then Sarah waved her hand.

"My favorite is the time we caught Josiah in our bear trap—William and me."

That wasn't Josiah's favorite, but he grinned good-naturedly along with the rest of them.

"Mine," Ezekiel said, chest puffed out like a pigeon, "was the time I kept the Putnam boys trapped so you all could escape. If I hadn't been there—"

"Good, then, Ezekiel," Hope said. "Who's next?"

"I'll never forget the time I had to stand up in court in Salem Town," William said.

Sarah stared at her brother. "That was your favorite? I was terrified!"

"So was I," William said. "But I've not been such a rabbit about things since then."

There was silence as everyone bobbed their heads and smiled at William.

Then Rachel said, "I will always remember every time we gave you boys the slip!"

"Which was never!" Ezekiel said.

"Which was always," Hope said. Her eyes sparkled at Ezekiel. "Did I ever tell you what an annoying boy you always were?"

Ezekiel wrinkled his nose at her. "There was no need," he said.

Hope laughed and then reached over to put her hand on Betty's arm. "What about you, Betty?"

Betty folded her pale little fingers under her chin and wrinkled her brow to think. Josiah had a special memory of her, poking her face up over the edge of her father's wagon and calling Josiah her rescuer while he pulled it out of the mud. But he would keep that one to himself. There would be no end to the teasing if Hope knew that.

"The map," Betty said finally. "I loved drawing the map."

"I hope so!" Rachel said. "Or we wouldn't be sitting here now. Josiah, tell us yours."

Josiah had started to hope no one would notice that he hadn't spoken yet, and he almost wished he hadn't started this game. There were so many pictures in his mind, sharply etched so they could never be erased. But he was afraid if he started to talk about them, the tears would only choke out his words.

"I think we have the same one," Hope said suddenly. She

was watching his face carefully as he struggled. "See if this isn't yours, too, Josiah." She looked around at all of them, her eyes shining, her arms outstretched on her lap as if she didn't want to close anyone off. "My favorite memory of the Merry Band," she said, "will always be this very moment. Look at us—each of us almost grown now, each of us so much taller and wiser than we were when first we met together. I shall never forget this night." She looked sideways at her brother. "Is that your favorite, too, Josiah?"

He smiled at her gratefully. "Aye," he said. "It is."

They laughed and ate Rachel's smuggled berry tarts until the "owl" hooted and Rachel and Ezekiel saw Betty home and Sarah and William walked with them as far as Fair Maid's Hill. There were no tears at any of the partings, for Hope had made them all promise to pretend that they were only saying good night—that surely they would meet on some secret mission tomorrow.

But Josiah knew that this time tomorrow, he and Hope would be getting ready for bed in Phillip English's house, and the next day they would walk up the gangplank of *The Hutchinson* with everything they owned. There would be no more secret missions for the Merry Band.

As they walked to Joseph Putnam's, where they would sleep that night before their journey to Salem Town at dawn, Hope stopped Josiah on the road.

"Betty gave me a message from Silas," she said.

"She still sees him, even though everyone knows she helped him?"

"Not anymore," Hope said sadly. "He's gone. They sent

him off to live with his mother's people in Marblehead. They said he wasn't fit to live here with the Putnams."

"He's lucky, then!" Josiah said.

"Aye." Hope walked on, but Josiah knew she had more to say. She was looking shyly down at her skirts. "He told Betty to tell me he would never forget me," she said softly. "And something else."

Please don't let it be anything else romantic, Josiah thought. *I couldn't bear it.*

"He said that you, Josiah, were the bravest man he ever knew."

They went the rest of the way in silence, and Josiah was glad for that. He was tired of talking and tired of acting as if he didn't have an ache in his chest that wouldn't go away.

He did forget about it for a moment or two, though, when they reached Joseph Putnam's parlor. There they found Phillip English standing at the fireplace, his elegant hair to his shoulders, and his kind smile lighting up the room.

"Who is this young man?" Phillip said to Papa when Josiah walked in.

"Our captain has grown, has he not?" Joseph Putnam said.

"I needn't have come, then," Phillip said. "This is as fine a man as any to help you escort your women to Salem Town tomorrow, Hutchinson!"

Papa smiled, and Josiah thought he saw a glint of pride in his eyes.

"What news have you from Salem Town, Phillip?" Papa said.

"Ah, some you'll surely be interested in. The magistrates of the court finally saw the Putnam boys today."

"They've been in the jail all these weeks?" Joseph Putnam said.

"Aye. You know Thomas Putnam tried to have the charges dismissed when they learned Hope and Josiah would not be testifying."

"So they'll be on their way back here tomorrow, eh?" Papa said gruffly.

"No, quite the opposite. The magistrates told Thomas Putnam that an attempt at murder could be easily proven, even without the victims there to tell their stories. They will use the depositions you provided, and they intend to bring young Silas in from Marblehead to tell his story. They agreed with you, Joseph. Haven't these children been through enough without having to appear in court and see their attackers again?" Phillip laughed his musical laugh. "No, the Putnam boys are back in the jail tonight, awaiting their official trial some days hence—and it's sure they'll be spending a great deal more time in those cells in the years to come."

"Do you think they'll be changed by all this?" Joseph Putnam said. "'Tis a pity, somehow. Eleazer is no older than Josiah. What life does he have ahead?"

"I think we can only pray that God will somehow intervene," Phillip said. "I suppose they will have plenty of time for prayer, since the magistrates predict they'll spend several years in jail."

Papa cleared his throat. "I have some happier news."

Josiah looked at him in surprise. He hadn't seen anything but worry and sadness on his father's face these last few weeks. Where could good news have come from?

"Phillip has presented me tonight with the reply to a letter

I asked him to send for me some weeks ago, when first I thought of moving the family to Virginia."

Papa drew the letter from inside his shirt and handed it to Josiah.

"Sir?" Josiah said.

"Open it. Read it."

Josiah's hands shook as he unfolded the distinguished-looking piece of parchment and studied the swirling flourishes of ink inside. It took him a moment to grow used to the handwriting, but when he did, his eyes widened and he looked at his father in disbelief.

"Read it aloud," Papa said.

"To Joseph Hutchinson, Salem Village, Massachusetts Colony," Josiah began. "We are pleased to inform you that your son, Josiah Hutchinson, has been accepted as a student at the Grammar School, College of William and Mary, Williamsburg, Virginia Colony. We greet the prospect of meeting this fine young student with much an-ti-ci-pation."

Josiah stumbled a little over the last word, but the burst of applause in the parlor covered that up.

"A real school, Captain!" Joseph Putnam said. "'Tis brand new, but I hear you'll get a fine education there."

Josiah held the letter in his hand and ran his fingers along the parchment. It was as if he held in his palm the chance to be everything these three men were.

It was late before the men put out the lamps and left the parlor. Papa and Phillip were yawning and went straight upstairs to bed, but Josiah dragged his feet as he climbed the steps. He wasn't sleepy at all, and he didn't look forward to lying awake thinking thoughts that made his chest hurt.

On the first landing, he was met by Joseph Putnam, who was on his way down with Daniel Josiah in his arms. Josiah looked at him curiously.

"I like to take him out on the porch for a few minutes each evening," Joseph explained. "I can tell him the important things in the quiet, you see."

"Oh," Josiah said.

"Would you like to join us, Captain? I think there are some things he needs to hear from you."

Josiah wasn't sure what he would say to a six-week-old baby, but he followed Joseph out to the porch and watched him tuck Daniel Josiah into the cradle carved with angels that Phillip and Mary English had given him.

He doesn't have much hair, Josiah thought. But the feathery fringe at the base of his head was the same oak color as his father's.

Josiah grinned to himself. Hope, of course, had asked him the other day if he thought Daniel Josiah would grow up to be as handsome as Joseph Putnam.

When Joseph finally sank back into his chair, he looked softly at Josiah. "You're somewhat saddened, Captain, for a man about to embark on a sea voyage, with a fine education ahead of him, eh?"

Josiah nodded soberly.

"Well, even though I think your father has made a wise choice for all of you, I am somewhat saddened myself. You have been a good friend to me, Captain."

Josiah's heart hurt so much that he thought it would break open. All he could do was nod.

"But there will always be a bond between us, eh?" Joseph said. He looked down at his sleeping baby. "Daniel Josiah and I have talked of it many times. You can write me long letters and send them by your father's ships to Phillip English, and I will send my replies back to you. I will have to report to you, of course."

"Report?" Josiah said.

"Aye, on Rachel and Ezekiel and William and Sarah. I am to watch over them for you, am I not?"

Josiah could feel a smile nudging at his mouth. "Aye," he said slowly.

"And I know someday, Captain, you will sail one of those ships up the coast yourself, right into Salem Harbor. You must!"

Josiah couldn't hold back a smile now. "Why?" he said.

"Because . . . I want you to make sure that I have raised Daniel Josiah to be as fine a man as you have become."

There was a magical silence. Little Daniel sighed in his cradle, and somehow the ache in Josiah's chest didn't seem quite so big.

The front door swung open, and Joseph Hutchinson stepped out, hair rumpled from his pillow.

"I thought you'd gone to bed," Joseph Putnam said.

"Ach, there will be no sleep for me tonight, I fear, unless I . . . " He stopped and looked at Josiah. "I've a mind to go for a walk. Will you join me, then?"

Josiah nodded eagerly and stood up. But before he followed his father down the steps, he turned and looked down at his namesake.

"You've naught to fear about becoming a man," he

whispered to the baby. "Just follow what your father does and I promise you—"

He didn't say any more, because the tears were coming. They were shining in Joseph Putnam's eyes, too, as Josiah exchanged grins with him and ran off after his father.

The Blessing Place was shimmering with moonlight when they got there, and Papa stood for a long time looking over all he was leaving behind.

Standing beside him, Josiah thought, *I wonder if he has a pain in his heart like I do?*

"Do you think me a coward, Josiah?" his father said suddenly.

Josiah nearly fell from the hill. "Why would I think that, sir?" he said.

Papa looked down at him. "I'm not staying to fight the fight. I am choosing to leave this church behind instead of working to my death to set it right."

For a moment, Josiah thought he was being put to a test, and he struggled to find the right answer. But as his father continued to look at him, his usually piercing blue eyes were full of the question he had just asked. He wanted an honest answer.

"Your decision," Josiah said slowly. "'Tis God's will, is it not?"

"Aye, but that does not mean others will see it that way. I care not what most men think—but you, Josiah, I care a great deal what you think of me."

Josiah thought his knees would give way under him, and he wanted to sit down. He had to plant his feet in the grass to keep standing beside his father.

"You see," Papa went on, "I do not see this move as giving up. God never wants us to beat our heads against a wall that will never move. Samuel Parris has good in him. You can see it in the way he cares for his daughter. But he is a weak man, and he does not go to God for strength. He will always be under the thumbs of men who are themselves ruled by fear. No, I see our move as going forward to do God's work. But it is important that you see that, too, or I do it all for nothing."

Their eyes met, and Josiah knew he would no longer have his father's stern, piercing gaze coming at him. Papa was looking at him now as he would look at Joseph Putnam or Phillip English. He was looking at him as a man, and he had to answer as a man.

"I see it, sir," Josiah said. "I know it is right. But there's a pain. . . ."

Joseph Hutchinson put a burly hand to Josiah's chest. "Here?" he said.

"Aye."

His father nodded and put his hand on his own chest. "It comes from looking back—on the things we've loved, the things we've come to cherish. But that's why I came to the Blessing Place tonight. I needed to remember that no matter where we go or what we do, there will always be people and things to love and cherish, because there is always God." He put his hand on Josiah's shoulder. "When God reminds us of that, the pain goes away in time."

Papa looked out over Salem Village for a moment, and then he looked back at Josiah with a shine in his eyes. "Will you move forward with me, son?" he said. "At my side?"

Josiah looked back at his father, and he knew he had a shine in his eyes, too. And a proud square to his shoulders. And no pain in his heart.

"Aye, sir. I will," Josiah said proudly. As they turned and left Salem Village behind in the darkness, he knew it was God's will, too.

A Map of
SALEM VILLAGE
& Vicinity in 1692

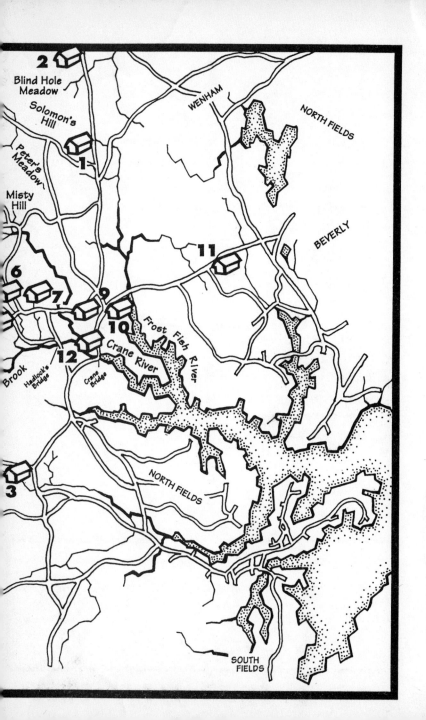